Bram Stoker

THE LAIR
OF THE
WHITE WORM

Bram Stoker (1847 – 1912)

Known now mainly for *Dracula* (1897), Abraham Stoker was firstly a theatrical manager of the Victorian actor and impresario Sir Henry Irving. His famous client's roles, which included playing sinister hypnotists, murderers, and the spectral Flying Dutchman, strongly influenced Bram Stoker's writing. His other works include *The Mystery of the Sea* (1902), *The Jewel of Seven Stars* (1907), *The Lady of the Shroud* (1909) and this book, *The Lair of the White Worm* (1911).

ISBN: 0-646-41842-4

First published: 1911
Copyright © Deodand Publishing, 2002

Published by Deodand Books, PO Box 3230, Norwood, 5067, AUSTRALIA.

D2002-008

CHAPTER I
ADAM SALTON ARRIVES

ADAM SALTON SAUNTERED INTO the Empire Club, Sydney, and found awaiting him a letter from his grand-uncle. He had first heard from the old gentleman less than a year before, when Richard Salton had claimed kinship, stating that he had been unable to write earlier, as he had found it very difficult to trace his grand-nephew's address. Adam was delighted and replied cordially; he had often heard his father speak of the older branch of the family with whom his people had long lost touch. Some interesting correspondence had ensued. Adam eagerly opened the letter which had only just arrived, and conveyed a cordial invitation to stop with his grand-uncle at Lesser Hill, for as long a time as he could spare.

"Indeed," Richard Salton went on, "I am in hopes that you will make your permanent home here. You see, my dear boy, you and I are all that remain of our race, and it is but fitting that you should succeed me when the time comes. In this year of grace, 1860, I am close on eighty years of age, and though we have been a long-lived race, the span of life cannot be prolonged beyond reasonable bounds. I am prepared to like you, and to make your home with me as happy as you could wish. So do come at once on receipt of this, and find the welcome I am waiting to give you. I send, in case such may make matters easy for you, a banker's draft for 200 pounds. Come soon, so that we may both of us enjoy many happy days together. If you are able to give me the pleasure of seeing you, send me as soon as you can a letter telling me when to expect you. Then when you arrive at Plymouth or Southampton or whatever port you are bound for, wait on board, and I will meet you at the earliest hour possible."

Old Mr. Salton was delighted when Adam's reply arrived and sent a groom hot-foot to his crony, Sir Nathaniel de Salis, to inform him that his grand-nephew was due at Southampton on the twelfth of June.

Mr. Salton gave instructions to have ready a carriage early on the important day, to start for Stafford, where he would catch the 11.40 a.m. train. He would stay that night with his grand-nephew, either on the ship, which would be a new experience for him, or, if his guest should prefer it, at a hotel. In either case they would start in the early morning for home. He had given instructions to his bailiff to send the postillion carriage on to Southampton, to be ready for their journey home, and to arrange for relays of his own horses to be sent on at once. He intended that his grand-nephew, who had been all his life in Australia, should see something of rural England on the drive. He had plenty of young horses of his own breeding and breaking, and could depend on a journey memorable to the young man. The luggage would be sent on by rail to Stafford, where one of his carts would meet it. Mr. Salton, during the journey to Southampton, often wondered if his grand-nephew was as much excited as he was at the idea of meeting so near a relation for the first time; and it was with an effort that he controlled himself. The endless railway lines and switches round the Southampton Docks fired his anxiety afresh.

As the train drew up on the dockside, he was getting his hand traps together, when the carriage door was wrenched open and a young man jumped in.

"How are you, uncle? I recognised you from the photo you sent me! I wanted to meet you as soon as I could, but everything is so strange to me that I didn't quite know what to do. However, here I am. I am glad to see you, sir. I have been dreaming of this happiness for thousands of miles; now I find that the reality beats all the dreaming!" As he spoke the old man and the young one were heartily wringing each other's hands.

The meeting so auspiciously begun proceeded well. Adam, seeing that the old man was interested in the novelty of the ship, suggested that he should stay the night on board, and that he would himself be ready to start at any hour and go anywhere that the other suggested. This affectionate willingness to fall in with his own plans quite won the old man's heart. He warmly accepted the invitation, and at once they became not only on terms of affectionate relationship, but almost like old friends. The heart of the old man, which had been empty for so long, found a new delight. The young man found, on landing in the old country, a welcome and a surrounding in full harmony with all his dreams throughout his wanderings and solitude, and the promise of a fresh and adventurous life. It was not long before the old man accepted him to full relationship by calling him by his Christian name. After a long talk on affairs of interest, they retired to the cabin, which the elder was to share. Richard Salton put his hands affectionately on the boy's shoulders – though Adam was in his twenty-seventh year, he was a boy, and always would be, to his grand-uncle.

"I am so glad to find you as you are, my dear boy – just such a young man as I had always hoped for as a son, in the days when I still had such hopes. However, that is all past. But thank God there is a new life to begin for both of us. To you must be the larger part – but there is still time for some of it to be shared in common. I have waited till we should have seen each other to enter upon the subject; for I thought it better not to tie up your young life to my old one till we should have sufficient personal

knowledge to justify such a venture. Now I can, so far as I am
concerned, enter into it freely, since from the moment my eyes
rested on you I saw my son – as he shall be, God willing – if he
chooses such a course himself."

"Indeed I do, sir – with all my heart!"

"Thank you, Adam, for that." The old man's eyes filled and his
voice trembled. Then, after a long silence between them, he went
on: "When I heard you were coming I made my will. It was well
that your interests should be protected from that moment on.
Here is the deed – keep it, Adam. All I have shall belong to you;
and if love and good wishes, or the memory of them, can make
life sweeter, yours shall be a happy one. Now, my dear boy, let us
turn in. We start early in the morning and have a long drive before
us. I hope you don't mind driving? I was going to have the old
travelling carriage in which my grandfather, your great-grand-
uncle, went to Court when William IV was king. It is all right –
they built well in those days – and it has been kept in perfect order. But I think I have done better: I have sent the carriage in
which I travel myself. The horses are of my own breeding, and
relays of them shall take us all the way. I hope you like horses?
They have long been one of my greatest interests in life."

"I love them, sir, and I am happy to say I have many of my
own. My father gave me a horse farm for myself when I was
eighteen. I devoted myself to it, and it has gone on. Before I
came away, my steward gave me a memorandum that we have in
my own place more than a thousand, nearly all good."

"I am glad, my boy. Another link between us."

"Just fancy what a delight it will be, sir, to see so much of England – and with you!"

"Thank you again, my boy. I will tell you all about your future
home and its surroundings as we go. We shall travel in old-
fashioned state, I tell you. My grandfather always drove four-in-
hand; and so shall we."

"Oh, thanks, sir, thanks. May I take the ribbons sometimes?"

"Whenever you choose, Adam. The team is your own. Every
horse we use to-day is to be your own."

"You are too generous, uncle!"

"Not at all. Only an old man's selfish pleasure. It is not every
day that an heir to the old home comes back. And – oh, by the
way. . . No, we had better turn in now – I shall tell you the rest in
the morning."

CHAPTER II
THE CASWALLS OF CASTRA REGIS

MR. SALTON HAD ALL HIS LIFE been an early riser, and necessarily an early waker. But early as he woke on the next morning – and although there was an excuse for not prolonging sleep in the constant whirr and rattle of the "donkey" engine winches of the great ship – he met the eyes of Adam fixed on him from his berth. His grand-nephew had given him the sofa, occupying the lower berth himself. The old man, despite his great strength and normal activity, was somewhat tired by his long journey of the day before, and the prolonged and exciting interview which followed it. So he was glad to lie still and rest his body, whilst his mind was actively exercised in taking in all he could of his strange surroundings. Adam, too, after the pastoral habit to which he had been bred, woke with the dawn, and was ready to enter on the experiences of the new day whenever it might suit his elder companion. It was little wonder, then, that, so soon as each realised the other's readiness, they simultaneously jumped up and began to dress. The steward had by previous instructions early breakfast prepared, and it was not long before they went down the gangway on shore in search of the carriage.

They found Mr. Salton's bailiff looking out for them on the dock, and he brought them at once to where the carriage was waiting in the street. Richard Salton pointed out with pride to his young companion the suitability of the vehicle for every need of travel. To it were harnessed four useful horses, with a postillion to each pair.

"See," said the old man proudly, "how it has all the luxuries of useful travel – silence and isolation as well as speed. There is nothing to obstruct the view of those travelling and no one to overhear what they may say. I have used that trap for a quarter of a century, and I never saw one more suitable for travel. You shall test it shortly. We are going to drive through the heart of England; and as we go I'll tell you what I was speaking of last night. Our route is to be by Salisbury, Bath, Bristol, Cheltenham, Worcester, Stafford; and so home."

Adam remained silent a few minutes, during which he seemed all eyes, for he perpetually ranged the whole circle of the horizon.

"Has our journey to-day, sir," he asked, "any special relation to what you said last night that you wanted to tell me?"

"Not directly; but indirectly, everything."

"Won't you tell me now – I see we cannot be overheard – and if anything strikes you as we go along, just run it in. I shall understand."

So old Salton spoke:

"To begin at the beginning, Adam. That lecture of yours on 'The Romans in Britain,' a report of which you posted to me, set me thinking – in addition to telling me your tastes. I wrote to you at once and asked you to come home, for it struck me that if you were fond of historical research – as seemed a fact – this was exactly the place for you, in addition to its being the home of your own forbears. If you could learn so much of the British Romans so far away in New South Wales, where there cannot be even a tradition of them, what might you not make of the same amount of study on the very spot. Where we are going is in the real heart of the old kingdom of Mercia, where there are traces of all the various nationalities which made up the conglomerate which became Britain."

"I rather gathered that you had some more definite – more personal reason for my hurrying. After all, history can keep – except in the making!"

"Quite right, my boy. I had a reason such as you very wisely guessed. I was anxious for you to be here when a rather important phase of our local history occurred."

"What is that, if I may ask, sir?"

"Certainly. The principal land-owner of our part of the county is on his way home, and there will be a great home-coming, which you may care to see. The fact is, for more than a century the various owners in the succession here, with the exception of a short time, have lived abroad."

"How is that, sir, if I may ask?"

"The great house and estate in our part of the world is Castra Regis, the family seat of the Caswall family. The last owner who lived here was Edgar Caswall, grandfather of the man who is coming here – and he was the only one who stayed even a short time. This man's grandfather, also named Edgar – they keep the tradition of the family Christian name – quarrelled with his family and went to live abroad, not keeping up any intercourse, good or bad, with his relatives, although this particular Edgar, as I told you, did visit his family estate, yet his son was born and lived and died abroad, while his grandson, the latest inheritor, was also born and lived abroad till he was over thirty – his present age. This was the second line of absentees. The great estate of Castra Regis has had no knowledge of its owner for five generations – covering more than a hundred and twenty years. It has been well administered, however, and no tenant or other connected with it has had anything of which to complain. All the same, there has been much natural anxiety to see the new owner, and we are all excited about the event of his coming. Even I am, though I own my own estate, which, though adjacent, is quite apart from Castra Regis –

Here we are now in new ground for you. That is the spire of Salisbury Cathedral, and when we leave that we shall be getting close to the old Roman county, and you will naturally want your eyes. So we shall shortly have to keep our minds on old Mercia. However, you need not be disappointed. My old friend, Sir Nathaniel de Salis, who, like myself, is a free-holder near Castra Regis – his estate, Doom Tower, is over the border of Derbyshire, on the Peak – is coming to stay with me for the festivities to welcome Edgar Caswall. He is just the sort of man you will like. He is devoted to history, and is President of the Mercian Archaeological Society. He knows more of our own part of the country, with its history and its people, than anyone else. I expect he will have arrived before us, and we three can have a long chat after dinner. He is also our local geologist and natural historian. So you and he will have many interests in common. Amongst other things he has a special knowledge of the Peak and its caverns, and knows all the old legends of prehistoric times."

They spent the night at Cheltenham, and on the following morning resumed their journey to Stafford. Adam's eyes were in constant employment, and it was not till Salton declared that they had now entered on the last stage of their journey, that he referred to Sir Nathaniel's coming.

As the dusk was closing down, they drove on to Lesser Hill, Mr. Salton's house. It was now too dark to see any details of their surroundings. Adam could just see that it was on the top of a hill, not quite so high as that which was covered by the Castle, on whose tower flew the flag, and which was all ablaze with moving lights, manifestly used in the preparations for the festivities on the morrow. So Adam deferred his curiosity till daylight. His grand-uncle was met at the door by a fine old man, who greeted him warmly.

"I came over early as you wished. I suppose this is your grand-nephew – I am glad to meet you, Mr. Adam Salton. I am Nathaniel de Salis, and your uncle is one of my oldest friends."

Adam, from the moment of their eyes meeting, felt as if they were already friends. The meeting was a new note of welcome to those that had already sounded in his ears.

The cordiality with which Sir Nathaniel and Adam met, made the imparting of information easy. Sir Nathaniel was a clever man of the world, who had travelled much, and within a certain area studied deeply. He was a brilliant conversationalist, as was to be expected from a successful diplomatist, even under unstimulating conditions. But he had been touched and to a certain extent fired by the younger man's evident admiration and willingness to learn from him. Accordingly the conversation, which began on the most friendly basis, soon warmed to an interest above proof, as the old man spoke of it next day to Richard Salton. He knew already that his old friend wanted his grand-nephew to learn all he could of the subject in hand, and so had during his journey from the Peak put his thoughts in sequence for narration and explanation. Accordingly, Adam had only to listen and he must learn much that he wanted to know. When dinner was over and the servants had withdrawn, leaving the three men at their wine, Sir Nathaniel began.

"I gather from your uncle – by the way, I suppose we had better speak of you as uncle and nephew, instead of going into exact relationship? In fact, your uncle is so old and dear a friend, that, with your permission, I shall drop formality with you altogether and speak of you and to you as Adam, as though you were his son."

"I should like," answered the young man, "nothing better!"

The answer warmed the hearts of both the old men, but, with the usual avoidance of Englishmen of emotional subjects personal to themselves, they instinctively returned to the previous question. Sir Nathaniel took the lead.

"I understand, Adam, that your uncle has posted you regarding the relationships of the Caswall family?"

"Partly, sir; but I understood that I was to hear minuter details from you – if you would be so good."

"I shall be delighted to tell you anything so far as my knowledge goes. Well, the first Caswall in our immediate record is an Edgar, head of the family and owner of the estate, who came into his kingdom just about the time that George III did. He had one son of about twenty-four. There was a violent quarrel between the two. No one of this generation has any idea of the cause; but, considering the family characteristics, we may take it for granted that though it was deep and violent, it was on the surface trivial.

"The result of the quarrel was that the son left the house without a reconciliation or without even telling his father where he was going. He never came back again. A few years after, he died, without having in the meantime exchanged a word or a letter with his father. He married abroad and left one son, who seems to have been brought up in ignorance of all belonging to him. The gulf between them appears to have been unbridgable; for in time this son married and in turn had a son, but neither joy nor sorrow brought the sundered together. Under such conditions no *rapprochement* was to be looked for, and an utter indifference, founded at best on ignorance, took the place of family affection – even on community of interests. It was only due to the watchfulness of the lawyers that the birth of this new heir was ever made known. He actually spent a few months in the ancestral home.

"After this the family interest merely rested on heirship of the estate. As no other children have been born to any of the newer generations in the intervening years, all hopes of heritage are now centred in the grandson of this man.

"Now, it will be well for you to bear in mind the prevailing characteristics of this race. These were well preserved and unchanging; one and all they are the same: cold, selfish, dominant, reckless of consequences in pursuit of their own will. It was not that they did not keep faith, though that was a matter which gave them little concern, but that they took care to think beforehand of what they should do in order to gain their own ends. If they should make a mistake, someone else should bear the burthen of it. This was so perpetually recurrent that it seemed to be a part of a fixed policy. It was no wonder that, whatever changes took place, they were always ensured in their own possessions. They were absolutely cold and hard by nature. Not one of them – so far as we have any knowledge – was ever known to be touched by the softer sentiments, to swerve from his purpose, or hold his hand in obedience to the dictates of his heart. The pictures and effigies of them all show their adherence to the early Roman type. Their eyes were full; their hair, of raven blackness, grew thick and close and curly. Their figures were massive and typical of strength.

"The thick black hair, growing low down on the neck, told of vast physical strength and endurance. But the most remarkable characteristic is the eyes. Black, piercing, almost unendurable, they seem to contain in themselves a remarkable will power which there is no gainsaying. It is a power that is partly racial and partly individual: a power impregnated with some mysterious quality, partly hypnotic, partly mesmeric, which seems to take away from eyes that meet them all power of resistance – nay, all power of wishing to resist. With eyes like those, set in that all-commanding face, one would need to be strong indeed to think of resisting the inflexible will that lay behind.

"You may think, Adam, that all this is imagination on my part, especially as I have never seen any of them. So it is, but imagination based on deep study. I have made use of all I know or can surmise logically regarding this strange race. With such strange compelling qualities, is it any wonder that there is abroad an idea that in the race there is some demoniac possession, which tends to a more definite belief that certain individuals have in the past sold themselves to the Devil?

"But I think we had better go to bed now. We have a lot to get through to-morrow, and I want you to have your brain clear, and all your susceptibilities fresh. Moreover, I want you to come with me for an early walk, during which we may notice, whilst the matter is fresh in our minds, the peculiar disposition of this place – not merely your grand-uncle's estate, but the lie of the country around it. There are many things on which we may seek – and perhaps find – enlightenment. The more we know at the start, the more things which may come into our view will develop themselves."

CHAPTER III

DIANA'S GROVE

CURIOSITY TOOK ADAM SALTON out of bed in the early morning, but when he had dressed and gone downstairs; he found that, early as he was, Sir Nathaniel was ahead of him. The old gentleman was quite prepared for a long walk, and they started at once.

Sir Nathaniel, without speaking, led the way to the east, down the hill. When they had descended and risen again, they found themselves on the eastern brink of a steep hill. It was of lesser height than that on which the Castle was situated; but it was so placed that it commanded the various hills that crowned the ridge. All along the ridge the rock cropped out, bare and bleak, but broken in rough natural castellation. The form of the ridge was a segment of a circle, with the higher points inland to the west. In the centre rose the Castle, on the highest point of all. Between the various rocky excrescences were groups of trees of various sizes and heights, amongst some of which were what, in the early morning light, looked like ruins. These – whatever they were – were of massive grey stone, probably limestone rudely cut – if indeed they were not shaped naturally. The fall of the ground was steep all along the ridge, so steep that here and there both trees and rocks and buildings seemed to overhang the plain far below, through which ran many streams.

Sir Nathaniel stopped and looked around, as though to lose nothing of the effect. The sun had climbed the eastern sky and was making all details clear. He pointed with a sweeping gesture, as though calling Adam's attention to the extent of the view. Having done so, he covered the ground more slowly, as though inviting attention to detail. Adam was a willing and attentive pupil, and followed his motions exactly, missing – or trying to miss – nothing.

"I have brought you here, Adam, because it seems to me that this is the spot on which to begin our investigations. You have now in front of you almost the whole of the ancient kingdom of Mercia. In fact, we see the whole of it except that furthest part, which is covered by the Welsh Marches and those parts which are hidden from where we stand by the high ground of the immediate west. We can see – theoretically – the whole of the eastern bound of the kingdom, which ran south from the Humber to the Wash. I want you to bear in mind the trend of the ground, for some time, sooner or later, we shall do well to have it in our mind's eye when we are considering the ancient traditions and superstitions, and are trying to find the *rationale* of them. Each legend, each superstition which we receive, will help in the understanding and possible elucidation of the others. And as all such have a local basis, we can come closer to the truth – or the probability – by knowing the local conditions as we go along. It will help us to bring to our aid such geological truth as we may have between us. For instance, the building materials used in various ages can afford their own lessons to understanding eyes. The very heights and shapes and materials of these hills – nay, even of the wide plain that lies between us and the sea – have in themselves the materials of enlightening books."

"For instance, sir?" said Adam, venturing a question.

"Well, look at those hills which surround the main one where the site for the Castle was wisely chosen – on the highest ground. Take the others. There is something ostensible in each of them, and in all probability something unseen and unproved, but to be imagined, also."

"For instance?" continued Adam.

"Let us take them *seriatim*. That to the east, where the trees are, lower down – that was once the location of a Roman temple, possibly founded on a pre-existing Druidical one. Its name implies the former, and the grove of ancient oaks suggests the latter."

"Please explain."

"The old name translated means 'Diana's Grove.' Then the next one higher than it, but just beyond it, is called '*Mercy*' – in all probability a corruption or familiarisation of the word *Mercia*, with a Roman pun included. We learn from early manuscripts that the place was called *Vilula Misericordiae*. It was originally a nunnery, founded by Queen Bertha, but done away with by King Penda, the reactionary to Paganism after St. Augustine. Then comes your uncle's place – Lesser Hill. Though it is so close to the Castle, it is not connected with it. It is a freehold, and, so far as we know, of equal age. It has always belonged to your family."

"Then there only remains the Castle!"

"That is all; but its history contains the histories of all the others – in fact, the whole history of early England." Sir Nathaniel, seeing the expectant look on Adam's face, went on:

"The history of the Castle has no beginning so far as we know. The furthest records or surmises or inferences simply accept it as existing. Some of these – guesses, let us call them – seem to show that there was some sort of structure there when the Romans came, therefore it must have been a place of importance in Druid times – if indeed that was the beginning. Naturally the Romans accepted it, as they did everything of the kind that was, or might be, useful. The change is shown or inferred in the name Castra. It was the highest protected ground, and so naturally became the most important of their camps. A study of the map will show you that it must have been a most important centre. It both protected the advances already made to the north, and helped to dominate the sea coast. It sheltered the western marches, beyond which lay savage Wales – and danger. It provided a means of getting to the Severn, round which lay the great Roman roads then coming into existence, and made possible the great waterway to the heart of England – through the Severn and its tributaries. It brought the east and the west together by the swiftest and easiest ways known to those times. And, finally, it provided means of descent on London and all the expanse of country watered by the Thames.

"With such a centre, already known and organised, we can easily see that each fresh wave of invasion – the Angles, the Saxons, the Danes, and the Normans – found it a desirable possession and so ensured its upholding. In the earlier centuries it was merely a vantage ground. But when the victorious Romans brought with them the heavy solid fortifications impregnable to the weapons of the time, its commanding position alone ensured its adequate building and equipment. Then it was that the fortified camp of the Caesars developed into the castle of the king. As we are as yet ignorant of the names of the first kings of Mercia, no historian has been able to guess which of them made it his ultimate defence; and I suppose we shall never know now. In process of time, as the arts of war developed, it increased in size and strength, and although recorded details are lacking, the history is written not merely in the stone of its building, but is inferred in the changes of structure. Then the sweeping changes which followed the Norman Conquest wiped out all lesser records than its own. To-day we must accept it as one of the earliest castles of the Conquest, probably not later than the time of Henry I. Roman and Norman were both wise in their retention of places of approved strength or utility. So it was that these surrounding heights, already established and to a certain extent proved, were retained. Indeed, such characteristics as already pertained to them were preserved, and to-day afford to us lessons regarding things which have themselves long since passed away.

"So much for the fortified heights; but the hollows too have their own story. But how the time passes! We must hurry home, or your uncle will wonder what has become of us."

He started with long steps towards Lesser Hill, and Adam was soon furtively running in order to keep up with him.

CHAPTER IV
THE LADY ARABELLA MARCH

"NOW, THERE IS NO HURRY, but so soon as you are both ready we shall start," Mr. Salton said when breakfast had begun. "I want to take you first to see a remarkable relic of Mercia, and then we'll go to Liverpool through what is called 'The Great Vale of Cheshire.' You may be disappointed, but take care not to prepare your mind" – this to Adam – "for anything stupendous or heroic. You would not think the place a vale at all, unless you were told so beforehand, and had confidence in the veracity of the teller. We should get to the Landing Stage in time to meet the *West African*, and catch Mr. Caswall as he comes ashore. We want to do him honour – and, besides, it will be more pleasant to have the introductions over before we go to his *fete* at the Castle."

The carriage was ready, the same as had been used the previous day, but there were different horses – magnificent animals, and keen for work. Breakfast was soon over, and they shortly took their places. The postillions had their orders, and were quickly on their way at an exhilarating pace.

Presently, in obedience to Mr. Salton's signal, the carriage drew up opposite a great heap of stones by the wayside.

"Here, Adam," he said, "is something that you of all men should not pass by unnoticed. That heap of stones brings us at once to the dawn of the Anglian kingdom. It was begun more than a thousand years ago – in the latter part of the seventh century – in memory of a murder. Wulfere, King of Mercia, nephew of Penda, here murdered his two sons for embracing Christianity. As was the custom of the time, each passer-by added a stone to the memorial heap. Penda represented heathen reaction after St. Augustine's mission. Sir Nathaniel can tell you as much as you want about this, and put you, if you wish, on the track of such accurate knowledge as there is."

Whilst they were looking at the heap of stones, they noticed that another carriage had drawn up beside them, and the passenger – there was only one – was regarding them curiously. The carriage was an old heavy travelling one, with arms blazoned on it gorgeously. The men took off their hats, as the occupant, a lady, addressed them.

"How do you do, Sir Nathaniel? How do you do, Mr. Salton? I hope you have not met with any accident. Look at me!"

As she spoke she pointed to where one of the heavy springs was broken across, the broken metal showing bright. Adam spoke up at once:

"Oh, that can soon be put right."

"Soon? There is no one near who can mend a break like that."

"I can."

"You!" She looked incredulously at the dapper young gentleman who spoke. "You – why, it's a workman's job."

"All right, I am a workman – though that is not the only sort of work I do. I am an Australian, and, as we have to move about fast, we are all trained to farriery and such mechanics as come into travel – I am quite at your service."

"I hardly know how to thank you for your kindness, of which I gladly avail myself. I don't know what else I can do, as I wish to meet Mr. Caswall of Castra Regis, who arrives home from Africa to-day. It is a notable home-coming; all the countryside want to do him honour." She looked at the old men and quickly made up her mind as to the identity of the stranger. "You must be Mr. Adam Salton of Lesser Hill. I am Lady Arabella March of Diana's Grove." As she spoke she turned slightly to Mr. Salton, who took the hint and made a formal introduction.

So soon as this was done, Adam took some tools from his uncle's carriage, and at once began work on the broken spring. He was an expert workman, and the breach was soon made good. Adam was gathering the tools which he had been using – which, after the manner of all workmen, had been scattered about – when he noticed that several black snakes had crawled out from the heap of stones and were gathering round him. This naturally occupied his mind, and he was not thinking of anything else when he noticed Lady Arabella, who had opened the door of the carriage, slip from it with a quick gliding motion. She was already among the snakes when he called out to warn her. But there seemed to be no need of warning. The snakes had turned and were wriggling back to the mound as quickly as they could. He laughed to himself behind his teeth as he whispered, "No need to fear there. They seem much more afraid of her than she of them." All the same he began to beat on the ground with a stick which was lying close to him, with the instinct of one used to such vermin. In an instant he was alone beside the mound with Lady Arabella, who appeared quite unconcerned at the incident. Then he took a long look at her, and her dress alone was sufficient to attract attention. She was clad in some kind of soft white stuff, which clung close to her form, showing to the full every movement of her sinuous figure. She wore a close-fitting cap of some fine fur of dazzling white. Coiled round her white throat was a large necklace of emeralds, whose profusion of colour dazzled when the sun shone on them. Her voice was peculiar, very low and sweet, and so soft that the dominant note was of sibilation. Her hands, too, were peculiar – long, flexible, white, with a strange movement as of waving gently to and fro.

She appeared quite at ease, and, after thanking Adam, said that if any of his uncle's party were going to Liverpool she would be most happy to join forces.

"Whilst you are staying here, Mr. Salton, you must look on the grounds of Diana's Grove as your own, so that you may come and go just as you do in Lesser Hill. There are some fine views, and not a few natural curiosities which are sure to interest you, if you are a student of natural history – specially of an earlier kind, when the world was younger."

The heartiness with which she spoke, and the warmth of her words – not of her manner, which was cold and distant – made him suspicious. In the meantime both his uncle and Sir Nathaniel had thanked her for the invitation – of which, however, they said they were unable to avail themselves. Adam had a suspicion that, though she answered regretfully, she was in reality relieved. When he had got into the carriage with the two old men, and they had driven off, he was not surprised when Sir Nathaniel spoke.

"I could not but feel that she was glad to be rid of us. She can play her game better alone!"

"What is her game?" asked Adam unthinkingly.

"All the county knows it, my boy. Caswall is a very rich man. Her husband was rich when she married him – or seemed to be. When he committed suicide, it was found that he had nothing left, and the estate was mortgaged up to the hilt. Her only hope is in a rich marriage. I suppose I need not draw any conclusion; you can do that as well as I can."

Adam remained silent nearly all the time they were travelling through the alleged Vale of Cheshire. He thought much during that journey and came to several conclusions, though his lips were unmoved. One of these conclusions was that he would be very careful about paying any attention to Lady Arabella. He was himself a rich man, how rich not even his uncle had the least idea, and would have been surprised had he known.

The remainder of the journey was uneventful, and upon arrival at Liverpool they went aboard the *West African*, which had just come to the landing-stage. There his uncle introduced himself to Mr. Caswall, and followed this up by introducing Sir Nathaniel and then Adam. The new-comer received them graciously, and said what a pleasure it was to be coming home after so long an absence of his family from their old seat. Adam was pleased at the warmth of the reception; but he could not avoid a feeling of repugnance at the man's face. He was trying hard to overcome this when a diversion was caused by the arrival of Lady Arabella. The diversion was welcome to all; the two Saltons and Sir Nathaniel were shocked at Caswall's face – so hard, so ruthless, so selfish, so dominant. "God help any," was the common thought, "who is under the domination of such a man!"

Presently his African servant approached him, and at once their thoughts changed to a larger toleration. Caswall looked indeed a savage – but a cultured savage. In him were traces of the softening civilisation of ages – of some of the higher instincts and education of man, no matter how rudimentary these might be. But the face of Oolanga, as his master called him, was unreformed, unsoftened savage, and inherent in it were all the hideous possibilities of a lost, devil-ridden child of the forest and the swamp – the lowest of all created things that could be regarded as in some form ostensibly human. Lady Arabella and Oolanga arrived almost simultaneously, and Adam was surprised to notice what effect their appearance had on each other. The woman seemed as if she would not – could not – condescend to exhibit any concern or interest in such a creature. On the other hand, the negro's bearing was such as in itself to justify her pride. He treated her not merely as a slave treats his master, but as a worshipper would treat a deity. He knelt before her with his hands out-stretched and his forehead in the dust. So long as she remained he did not move; it was only when she went over to Caswall that he relaxed his attitude of devotion and stood by respectfully.

Adam spoke to his own man, Davenport, who was standing by, having arrived with the bailiff of Lesser Hill, who had followed Mr. Salton in a pony trap. As he spoke, he pointed to an attentive ship's steward, and presently the two men were conversing.

"I think we ought to be moving," Mr. Salton said to Adam. "I have some things to do in Liverpool, and I am sure that both Mr. Caswall and Lady Arabella would like to get under weigh for Castra Regis."

"I too, sir, would like to do something," replied Adam. "I want to find out where Ross, the animal merchant, lives – I want to take a small animal home with me, if you don't mind. He is only a little thing, and will be no trouble."

"Of course not, my boy. What kind of animal is it that you want?"

"A mongoose."

"A mongoose! What on earth do you want it for?"

"To kill snakes."

"Good!" The old man remembered the mound of stones. No explanation was needed.

When Ross heard what was wanted, he asked:

"Do you want something special, or will an ordinary mongoose do?"

"Well, of course I want a good one. But I see no need for anything special. It is for ordinary use."

"I can let you have a choice of ordinary ones. I only asked, because I have in stock a very special one which I got lately from Nepaul. He has a record of his own. He killed a king cobra that had been seen in the Rajah's garden. But I don't suppose we have any snakes of the kind in this cold climate – I daresay an ordinary one will do."

When Adam got back to the carriage, carefully carrying the box with the mongoose, Sir Nathaniel said: "Hullo! what have you got there?"

"A mongoose."

"What for?"

"To kill snakes!"

Sir Nathaniel laughed.

"I heard Lady Arabella's invitation to you to come to Diana's Grove."

"Well, what on earth has that got to do with it?"

"Nothing directly that I know of. But we shall see." Adam waited, and the old man went on: "Have you by any chance heard the other name which was given long ago to that place."

"No, sir."

"It was called – Look here, this subject wants a lot of talking over. Suppose we wait till we are alone and have lots of time before us."

"All right, sir." Adam was filled with curiosity, but he thought it better not to hurry matters. All would come in good time. Then the three men returned home, leaving Mr. Caswall to spend the night in Liverpool.

The following day the Lesser Hill party set out for Castra Regis, and for the time Adam thought no more of Diana's Grove or of what mysteries it had contained – or might still contain.

The guests were crowding in, and special places were marked for important people. Adam, seeing so many persons of varied degree, looked round for Lady Arabella, but could not locate her. It was only when he saw the old-fashioned travelling carriage approach and heard the sound of cheering which went with it, that he realised that Edgar Caswall had arrived. Then, on looking more closely, he saw that Lady Arabella, dressed as he had seen her last, was seated beside him. When the carriage drew up at the great flight of steps, the host jumped down and gave her his hand.

It was evident to all that she was the chief guest at the festivities. It was not long before the seats on the dais were filled, while the tenants and guests of lesser importance had occupied all the coigns of vantage not reserved. The order of the day had been carefully arranged by a committee. There were some speeches, happily neither many nor long; and then festivities were suspended till the time for feasting arrived. In the interval Caswall walked among his guests, speaking to all in a friendly manner and expressing a general welcome. The other guests came down from the dais and followed his example, so there was unceremonious meeting and greeting between gentle and simple.

Adam Salton naturally followed with his eyes all that went on within their scope, taking note of all who seemed to afford any interest. He was young and a man and a stranger from a far distance; so on all these accounts he naturally took stock rather of the women than of the men, and of these, those who were young and attractive. There were lots of pretty girls among the crowd, and Adam, who was a handsome young man and well set up, got his full share of admiring glances. These did not concern him much, and he remained unmoved until there came along a group of three, by their dress and bearing, of the farmer class. One was a sturdy old man; the other two were good-looking girls, one of a little over twenty, the other not quite so old. So soon as Adam's eyes met those of the younger girl, who stood nearest to him, some sort of electricity flashed – that divine spark which begins by recognition, and ends in obedience. Men call it "Love."

Both his companions noticed how much Adam was taken by the pretty girl, and spoke of her to him in a way which made his heart warm to them.

"Did you notice that party that passed? The old man is Michael Watford, one of the tenants of Mr. Caswall. He occupies Mercy Farm, which Sir Nathaniel pointed out to you to-day. The girls are his grand-daughters, the elder, Lilla, being the only child of his elder son, who died when she was less than a year old. His wife died on the same day. She is a good girl – as good as she is pretty. The other is her first cousin, the daughter of Watford's second son. He went for a soldier when he was just over twenty, and was drafted abroad. He was not a good correspondent, though he was a good enough son. A few letters came, and then his father heard from the colonel of his regiment that he had been killed by dacoits in Burmah. He heard from the same source that his boy had been married to a Burmese, and that there was a daughter only a year old. Watford had the child brought home, and she grew up beside Lilla. The only thing that they heard of her birth was that her name was Mimi. The two children adored each other, and do to this day. Strange how different they are! Lilla all fair, like the old Saxon stock from which she is sprung; Mimi showing a trace of her mother's race. Lilla is as gentle as a dove, but Mimi's black eyes can glow whenever she is upset. The only thing that upsets her is when anything happens to injure or threaten or annoy Lilla. Then her eyes glow as do the eyes of a bird when her young are menaced."

CHAPTER V
THE WHITE WORM

MR. SALTON INTRODUCED ADAM to Mr. Watford and his grand-daughters, and they all moved on together. Of course neighbours in the position of the Watfords knew all about Adam Salton, his relationship, circumstances, and prospects. So it would have been strange indeed if both girls did not dream of possibilities of the future. In agricultural England, eligible men of any class are rare. This particular man was specially eligible, for he did not belong to a class in which barriers of caste were strong. So when it began to be noticed that he walked beside Mimi Watford and seemed to desire her society, all their friends endeavoured to give the promising affair a helping hand. When the gongs sounded for the banquet, he went with her into the tent where her grandfather had seats. Mr. Salton and Sir Nathaniel noticed that the young man did not come to claim his appointed place at the dais table; but they understood and made no remark, or indeed did not seem to notice his absence.

Lady Arabella sat as before at Edgar Caswall's right hand. She was certainly a striking and unusual woman, and to all it seemed fitting from her rank and personal qualities that she should be the chosen partner of the heir on his first appearance. Of course nothing was said openly by those of her own class who were present; but words were not necessary when so much could be expressed by nods and smiles. It seemed to be an accepted thing that at last there was to be a mistress of Castra Regis, and that she was present amongst them. There were not lacking some who, whilst admitting all her charm and beauty, placed her in the second rank, Lilla Watford being marked as first. There was sufficient divergence of type, as well as of individual beauty, to allow of fair comment; Lady Arabella represented the aristocratic type, and Lilla that of the commonalty.

When the dusk began to thicken, Mr. Salton and Sir Nathaniel walked home – the trap had been sent away early in the day – leaving Adam to follow in his own time. He came in earlier than was expected, and seemed upset about something. Neither of the elders made any comment. They all lit cigarettes, and, as dinner-time was close at hand, went to their rooms to get ready.

Adam had evidently been thinking in the interval. He joined the others in the drawing-room, looking ruffled and impatient – a condition of things seen for the first time. The others, with the patience – or the experience – of age, trusted to time to unfold and explain things. They had not long to wait. After sitting down and standing up several times, Adam suddenly burst out.

"That fellow seems to think he owns the earth. Can't he let people alone! He seems to think that he has only to throw his handkerchief to any woman, and be her master."

This outburst was in itself enlightening. Only thwarted affection in some guise could produce this feeling in an amiable young man. Sir Nathaniel, as an old diplomatist, had a way of understanding, as if by foreknowledge, the true inwardness of things, and asked suddenly, but in a matter-of-fact, indifferent voice:

"Was he after Lilla?"

"Yes, and the fellow didn't lose any time either. Almost as soon as they met, he began to butter her up, and tell her how beautiful she was. Why, before he left her side, he had asked himself to tea to-morrow at Mercy Farm. Stupid ass! He might see that the girl isn't his sort! I never saw anything like it. It was just like a hawk and a pigeon."

As he spoke, Sir Nathaniel turned and looked at Mr. Salton – a keen look which implied a full understanding.

"Tell us all about it, Adam. There are still a few minutes before dinner, and we shall all have better appetites when we have come to some conclusion on this matter."

"There is nothing to tell, sir; that is the worst of it. I am bound to say that there was not a word said that a human being could object to. He was very civil, and all that was proper – just what a landlord might be to a tenant's daughter. . . Yet – yet – well, I don't know how it was, but it made my blood boil."

"How did the hawk and the pigeon come in?" Sir Nathaniel's voice was soft and soothing, nothing of contradiction or overdone curiosity in it – a tone eminently suited to win confidence.

"I can hardly explain. I can only say that he looked like a hawk and she like a dove – and, now that I think of it, that is what they each did look like; and do look like in their normal condition."

"That is so!" came the soft voice of Sir Nathaniel.

Adam went on:

"Perhaps that early Roman look of his set me off. But I wanted to protect her; she seemed in danger."

"She seems in danger, in a way, from all you young men. I couldn't help noticing the way that even you looked – as if you wished to absorb her!"

"I hope both you young men will keep your heads cool," put in Mr. Salton. "You know, Adam, it won't do to have any quarrel between you, especially so soon after his home-coming and your arrival here. We must think of the feelings and happiness of our neighbours; mustn't we?"

"I hope so, sir. I assure you that, whatever may happen, or even threaten, I shall obey your wishes in this as in all things."

"Hush!" whispered Sir Nathaniel, who heard the servants in the passage bringing dinner.

After dinner, over the walnuts and the wine, Sir Nathaniel returned to the subject of the local legends.

"It will perhaps be a less dangerous topic for us to discuss than more recent ones."

"All right, sir," said Adam heartily. "I think you may depend on me now with regard to any topic. I can even discuss Mr. Caswall. Indeed, I may meet him to-morrow. He is going, as I said, to call at Mercy Farm at three o'clock – but I have an appointment at two."

"I notice," said Mr. Salton, "that you do not lose any time."

The two old men once more looked at each other steadily. Then, lest the mood of his listener should change with delay, Sir Nathaniel began at once:

"I don't propose to tell you all the legends of Mercia, or even to make a selection of them. It will be better, I think, for our purpose if we consider a few facts – recorded or unrecorded – about this neighbourhood. I think we might begin with Diana's Grove. It has roots in the different epochs of our history, and each has its special crop of legend. The Druid and the Roman are too far off for matters of detail; but it seems to me the Saxon and the Angles are near enough to yield material for legendary lore. We find that this particular place had another name besides Diana's Grove. This was manifestly of Roman origin, or of Grecian accepted as Roman. The other is more pregnant of adventure and romance than the Roman name. In Mercian tongue it was 'The Lair of the White Worm.' This needs a word of explanation at the beginning.

"In the dawn of the language, the word 'worm' had a somewhat different meaning from that in use to-day. It was an adaptation of the Anglo-Saxon 'wyrm,' meaning a dragon or snake; or from the Gothic 'waurms,' a serpent; or the Icelandic 'ormur,' or the German 'wurm.' We gather that it conveyed originally an idea of size and power, not as now in the diminutive of both these meanings. Here legendary history helps us. We have the well-known legend of the 'Worm Well' of Lambton Castle, and that of the 'Laidly Worm of Spindleston Heugh' near Bamborough. In both these legends the 'worm' was a monster of vast size and power – a veritable dragon or serpent, such as legend attributes to vast fens or quags where there was illimitable room for expansion. A glance at a geological map will show that whatever truth there may have been of the actuality of such monsters in the early geologic periods, at least there was plenty of possibility. In England there were originally vast plains where the plentiful supply of water could gather. The streams were deep and slow, and there were holes of abysmal depth, where any kind and size of antediluvian monster could find a habitat. In places, which now we can see from our windows, were mud-holes a hundred or more feet deep. Who can tell us when the age of the monsters which flourished in slime came to an end? There must have been places and conditions which made for greater longevity, greater size, greater strength than was usual. Such over-lappings may have come down even to our earlier centuries. Nay, are there not now creatures of a vastness of bulk regarded by the generality of men as impossible? Even in our own day there are seen the traces of animals, if not the animals themselves, of stupendous size – veritable survivals from earlier ages, preserved by some special qualities in their habitats. I remember meeting a distinguished man in India, who had the reputation of being a great shikaree, who told me that the greatest temptation he had ever had in his life was to shoot a giant snake which he had come across in the Terai of Upper India. He was on a tiger-shooting expedition, and as his elephant was crossing a nullah, it squealed. He looked down from his howdah and saw that the elephant had stepped across the body of a snake which was dragging itself through the jungle. 'So far as I could see,' he said, 'it must have been eighty or one hundred feet in length. Fully forty or fifty feet was on each side of the track, and though the weight which it dragged had thinned it, it was as thick round as a man's body. I suppose you know that when you are after tiger, it is a point of honour not to shoot at anything else, as life may depend on it. I could easily have spined this monster, but I felt that I must not – so, with regret, I had to let it go.'

"Just imagine such a monster anywhere in this country, and at once we could get a sort of idea of the 'worms,' which possibly did frequent the great morasses which spread round the mouths of many of the great European rivers."

"I haven't the least doubt, sir, that there may have been such monsters as you have spoken of still existing at a much later period than is generally accepted," replied Adam. "Also, if there were such things, that this was the very place for them. I have tried to think over the matter since you pointed out the configuration of the ground. But it seems to me that there is a hiatus somewhere. Are there not mechanical difficulties?"

"In what way?"

"Well, our antique monster must have been mighty heavy, and the distances he had to travel were long and the ways difficult. From where we are now sitting down to the level of the mud-holes is a distance of several hundred feet – I am leaving out of consideration altogether any lateral distance. Is it possible that there was a way by which a monster could travel up and down, and yet no chance recorder have ever seen him? Of course we have the legends; but is not some more exact evidence necessary in a scientific investigation?"

"My dear Adam, all you say is perfectly right, and, were we starting on such an investigation, we could not do better than follow your reasoning. But, my dear boy, you must remember that all this took place thousands of years ago. You must remember, too, that all records of the kind that would help us are lacking. Also, that the places to be considered were desert, so far as human habitation or population are considered. In the vast desolation of such a place as complied with the necessary conditions, there must have been such profusion of natural growth as would bar the progress of men formed as we are. The lair of such a monster would not have been disturbed for hundreds – or thousands – of years. Moreover, these creatures must have occupied places quite inaccessible to man. A snake who could make himself comfortable in a quagmire, a hundred feet deep, would be protected on the outskirts by such stupendous morasses as now no longer exist, or which, if they exist anywhere at all, can be on very few places on the earth's surface. Far be it from me to say that in more elemental times such things could not have been. The condition belongs to the geologic age – the great birth and growth of the world, when natural forces ran riot, when the struggle for existence was so savage that no vitality which was not founded in a gigantic form could have even a possibility of survival. That such a time existed, we have evidences in geology, but there only; we can never expect proofs such as this age demands. We can only imagine or surmise such things – or such conditions and such forces as overcame them."

CHAPTER VI

HAWK AND PIGEON

AT BREAKFAST-TIME NEXT MORNING Sir Nathaniel and Mr. Salton were seated when Adam came hurriedly into the room.

"Any news?" asked his uncle mechanically.

"Four."

"Four what?" asked Sir Nathaniel.

"Snakes," said Adam, helping himself to a grilled kidney.

"Four snakes. I don't understand."

"Mongoose," said Adam, and then added explanatorily: "I was out with the mongoose just after three."

"Four snakes in one morning! Why, I didn't know there were so many on the Brow" – the local name for the western cliff. "I hope that wasn't the consequence of our talk of last night?"

"It was, sir. But not directly."

"But, God bless my soul, you didn't expect to get a snake like the Lambton worm, did you? Why, a mongoose, to tackle a monster like that – if there were one – would have to be bigger than a haystack."

"These were ordinary snakes, about as big as a walking-stick."

"Well, it's pleasant to be rid of them, big or little. That is a good mongoose, I am sure; he'll clear out all such vermin round here," said Mr. Salton.

Adam went quietly on with his breakfast. Killing a few snakes in a morning was no new experience to him. He left the room the moment breakfast was finished and went to the study that his uncle had arranged for him. Both Sir Nathaniel and Mr. Salton took it that he wanted to be by himself, so as to avoid any questioning or talk of the visit that he was to make that afternoon. They saw nothing further of him till about half-an-hour before dinner-time. Then he came quietly into the smoking-room, where Mr. Salton and Sir Nathaniel were sitting together, ready dressed.

"I suppose there is no use waiting. We had better get it over at once," remarked Adam.

His uncle, thinking to make things easier for him, said: "Get what over?"

There was a sign of shyness about him at this. He stammered a little at first, but his voice became more even as he went on.

"My visit to Mercy Farm."

Mr. Salton waited eagerly. The old diplomatist simply smiled.

"I suppose you both know that I was much interested yesterday in the Watfords?" There was no denial or fending off the question. Both the old men smiled acquiescence. Adam went on: "I meant you to see it – both of you. You, uncle, because you are my uncle and the nearest of my own kin, and, moreover, you couldn't have been more kind to me or made me more welcome if you had been my own father." Mr. Salton said nothing. He simply held out his hand, and the other took it and held it for a few seconds. "And you, sir, because you have shown me something of the same affection which in my wildest dreams of home I had no right to expect." He stopped for an instant, much moved.

Sir Nathaniel answered softly, laying his hand on the youth's shoulder.

"You are right, my boy; quite right. That is the proper way to look at it. And I may tell you that we old men, who have no children of our own, feel our hearts growing warm when we hear words like those."

Then Adam hurried on, speaking with a rush, as if he wanted to come to the crucial point.

"Mr. Watford had not come in, but Lilla and Mimi were at home, and they made me feel very welcome. They have all a great regard for my uncle. I am glad of that any way, for I like them all – much. We were having tea, when Mr. Caswall came to the door, attended by the negro. Lilla opened the door herself. The window of the living-room at the farm is a large one, and from within you cannot help seeing anyone coming. Mr. Caswall said he had ventured to call, as he wished to make the acquaintance of all his tenants, in a less formal way, and more individually, than had been possible to him on the previous day. The girls made him welcome – they are very sweet girls those, sir; someone will be very happy some day there – with either of them."

"And that man may be you, Adam," said Mr. Salton heartily.

A sad look came over the young man's eyes, and the fire his uncle had seen there died out. Likewise the timbre left his voice, making it sound lonely.

"Such might crown my life. But that happiness, I fear, is not for me – or not without pain and loss and woe."

"Well, it's early days yet!" cried Sir Nathaniel heartily.

The young man turned on him his eyes, which had now grown excessively sad.

"Yesterday – a few hours ago – that remark would have given me new hope – new courage; but since then I have learned too much."

The old man, skilled in the human heart, did not attempt to argue in such a matter.

"Too early to give in, my boy."

"I am not of a giving-in kind," replied the young man earnestly. "But, after all, it is wise to realise a truth. And when a man, though he is young, feels as I do – as I have felt ever since yesterday, when I first saw Mimi's eyes – his heart jumps. He does not need to learn things. He knows."

There was silence in the room, during which the twilight stole on imperceptibly. It was Adam who again broke the silence.

"Do you know, uncle, if we have any second sight in our family?"

"No, not that I ever heard about. Why?"

"Because," he answered slowly, "I have a conviction which seems to answer all the conditions of second sight."

"And then?" asked the old man, much perturbed.

"And then the usual inevitable. What in the Hebrides and other places, where the Sight is a cult – a belief – is called 'the doom' – the court from which there is no appeal. I have often heard of second sight – we have many western Scots in Australia; but I have realised more of its true inwardness in an instant of this afternoon than I did in the whole of my life previously – a granite wall stretching up to the very heavens, so high and so dark that the eye of God Himself cannot see beyond. Well, if the Doom must come, it must. That is all."

The voice of Sir Nathaniel broke in, smooth and sweet and grave.

"Can there not be a fight for it? There can for most things."

"For most things, yes, but for the Doom, no. What a man can do I shall do. There will be – must be – a fight. When and where and how I know not, but a fight there will be. But, after all, what is a man in such a case?"

"Adam, there are three of us." Salton looked at his old friend as he spoke, and that old friend's eyes blazed.

"Ay, three of us," he said, and his voice rang.

There was again a pause, and Sir Nathaniel endeavoured to get back to less emotional and more neutral ground.

"Tell us of the rest of the meeting. Remember we are all pledged to this. It is a fight *e l'outrance*, and we can afford to throw away or forgo no chance."

"We shall throw away or lose nothing that we can help. We fight to win, and the stake is a life – perhaps more than one – we shall see." Then he went on in a conversational tone, such as he had used when he spoke of the coming to the farm of Edgar Caswall: "When Mr. Caswall came in, the negro went a short distance away and there remained. It gave me the idea that he expected to be called, and intended to remain in sight, or within hail. Then Mimi got another cup and made fresh tea, and we all went on together."

"Was there anything uncommon – were you all quite friendly?" asked Sir Nathaniel quietly.

"Quite friendly. There was nothing that I could notice out of the common – except," he went on, with a slight hardening of the voice, "except that he kept his eyes fixed on Lilla, in a way which was quite intolerable to any man who might hold her dear."

"Now, in what way did he look?" asked Sir Nathaniel.

"There was nothing in itself offensive; but no one could help noticing it."

"You did. Miss Watford herself, who was the victim, and Mr. Caswall, who was the offender, are out of range as witnesses. Was there anyone else who noticed?"

"Mimi did. Her face flamed with anger as she saw the look."

"What kind of look was it? Over-ardent or too admiring, or what? Was it the look of a lover, or one who fain would be? You understand?"

"Yes, sir, I quite understand. Anything of that sort I should of course notice. It would be part of my preparation for keeping my self-control – to which I am pledged."

"If it were not amatory, was it threatening? Where was the offence?"

Adam smiled kindly at the old man.

"It was not amatory. Even if it was, such was to be expected. I should be the last man in the world to object, since I am myself an offender in that respect. Moreover, not only have I been taught

to fight fair, but by nature I believe I am just. I would be as toler-
ant of and as liberal to a rival as I should expect him to be to me.
No, the look I mean was nothing of that kind. And so long as it
did not lack proper respect, I should not of my own part condescend to notice it. Did you ever study the eyes of a hound?"

"At rest?"

"No, when he is following his instincts! Or, better still," Adam
went on, "the eyes of a bird of prey when he is following his instincts. Not when he is swooping, but merely when he is watching
his quarry?"

"No," said Sir Nathaniel, "I don't know that I ever did. Why,
may I ask?"

"That was the look. Certainly not amatory or anything of that
kind – yet it was, it struck me, more dangerous, if not so deadly as
an actual threatening."

Again there was a silence, which Sir Nathaniel broke as he stood
up:

"I think it would be well if we all thought over this by ourselves.
Then we can renew the subject."

CHAPTER VII

OOLANGA

MR. SALTON HAD AN APPOINTMENT for six o'clock at Liverpool.
When he had driven off, Sir Nathaniel took Adam by the arm.

"May I come with you for a while to your study? I want to
speak to you privately without your uncle knowing about it, or
even what the subject is. You don't mind, do you? It is not idle
curiosity. No, no. It is on the subject to which we are all committed."

"Is it necessary to keep my uncle in the dark about it? He might
be offended."

"It is not necessary; but it is advisable. It is for his sake that I
asked. My friend is an old man, and it might concern him unduly
– even alarm him. I promise you there shall be nothing that could
cause him anxiety in our silence, or at which he could take um-
brage."

"Go on, sir!" said Adam simply.

"You see, your uncle is now an old man. I know it, for we were
boys together. He has led an uneventful and somewhat self-
contained life, so that any such condition of things as has now
arisen is apt to perplex him from its very strangeness. In fact, any
new matter is trying to old people. It has its own disturbances and
its own anxieties, and neither of these things are good for lives
that should be restful. Your uncle is a strong man, with a very
happy and placid nature. Given health and ordinary conditions of

life, there is no reason why he should not live to be a hundred. You and I, therefore, who both love him, though in different ways, should make it our business to protect him from all disturbing influences. I am sure you will agree with me that any labour to this end would be well spent. All right, my boy! I see your answer in your eyes; so we need say no more of that. And now," here his voice changed, "tell me all that took place at that interview. There are strange things in front of us – how strange we cannot at present even guess. Doubtless some of the difficult things to understand which lie behind the veil will in time be shown to us to see and to understand. In the meantime, all we can do is to work patiently, fearlessly, and unselfishly, to an end that we think is right. You had got so far as where Lilla opened the door to Mr. Caswall and the negro. You also observed that Mimi was disturbed in her mind at the way Mr. Caswall looked at her cousin."

"Certainly – though 'disturbed' is a poor way of expressing her objection."

"Can you remember well enough to describe Caswall's eyes, and how Lilla looked, and what Mimi said and did? Also Oolanga, Caswall's West African servant."

"I'll do what I can, sir. All the time Mr. Caswall was staring, he kept his eyes fixed and motionless – but not as if he was in a trance. His forehead was wrinkled up, as it is when one is trying to see through or into something. At the best of times his face has not a gentle expression; but when it was screwed up like that it was almost diabolical. It frightened poor Lilla so that she trembled, and after a bit got so pale that I thought she had fainted. However, she held up and tried to stare back, but in a feeble kind of way. Then Mimi came close and held her hand. That braced her up, and – still, never ceasing her return stare – she got colour again and seemed more like herself."

"Did he stare too?"

"More than ever. The weaker Lilla seemed, the stronger he became, just as if he were feeding on her strength. All at once she turned round, threw up her hands, and fell down in a faint. I could not see what else happened just then, for Mimi had thrown herself on her knees beside her and hid her from me. Then there was something like a black shadow between us, and there was the negro,* looking more like a malignant devil than ever. I am not usually a patient man, and the sight of that ugly devil is enough to make one's blood boil. When he saw my face, he seemed to realise danger – immediate danger – and slunk out of the room as noiselessly as if he had been blown out. I learned one thing, however – he is an enemy, if ever a man had one."

"That still leaves us three to two!" put in Sir Nathaniel.

"Then Caswall slunk out, much as the negro* had done. When

he had gone, Lilla recovered at once."

"Now," said Sir Nathaniel, anxious to restore peace, "have you found out anything yet regarding the negro? I am anxious to be posted regarding him. I fear there will be, or may be, grave trouble with him."

"Yes, sir, I've heard a good deal about him – of course it is not official; but hearsay must guide us at first. You know my man Davenport – private secretary, confidential man of business, and general factotum. He is devoted to me, and has my full confidence. I asked him to stay on board the *West African* and have a good look round, and find out what he could about Mr. Caswall. Naturally, he was struck with the aboriginal savage. He found one of the ship's stewards, who had been on the regular voyages to South Africa. He knew Oolanga and had made a study of him. He is a man who gets on well with blacks,* and they open their hearts to him. It seems that this Oolanga is quite a great person in the native* world of the African West Coast. He has the two things which men of his own colour respect: he can make them afraid, and he is lavish with money. I don't know whose money – but that does not matter. They are always ready to trumpet his greatness. Evil greatness it is – but neither does that matter. Briefly, this is his history. He was originally a witch-finder – about as low an occupation as exists amongst aboriginal savages. Then he got up in the world and became an Obi-man, which gives an opportunity to wealth *via* blackmail. Finally, he reached the highest honour in hellish service. He became a user of Voodoo, which seems to be a service of the utmost baseness and cruelty. I was told some of his deeds of cruelty, which are simply sickening. They made me long for an opportunity of helping to drive him back to hell. You might think to look at him that you could measure in some way the extent of his vileness; but it would be a vain hope. Monsters such as he is belong to an earlier and more rudimentary stage of barbarism. He is in his way a clever fellow – for a native;* but is none the less dangerous or the less hateful for that. The men in the ship told me that he was a collector: some of them had seen his collections. Such collections! All that was potent for evil in bird or beast, or even in fish. Beaks that could break and rend and tear – all the birds represented were of a predatory kind. Even the fishes are those which are born to destroy, to wound, to torture. The collection, I assure you, was an object lesson in human malignity. This being has enough evil in his face to frighten even a strong man. It is little wonder that the sight of it put that poor girl into a dead faint!"

Nothing more could be done at the moment, so they separated.

Adam was up in the early morning and took a smart walk round the Brow. As he was passing Diana's Grove, he looked in on the short avenue of trees, and noticed the snakes killed on the previous morning by the mongoose. They all lay in a row, straight and rigid, as if they had been placed by hands. Their skins seemed damp and sticky, and they were covered all over with ants and other insects. They looked loathsome, so after a glance, he passed on.

A little later, when his steps took him, naturally enough, past the entrance to Mercy Farm, he was passed by the negro, moving quickly under the trees wherever there was shadow. Laid across one extended arm, looking like dirty towels across a rail, he had the horrid-looking snakes. He did not seem to see Adam. No one was to be seen at Mercy except a few workmen in the farmyard, so, after waiting on the chance of seeing Mimi, Adam began to go slowly home.

Once more he was passed on the way. This time it was by Lady Arabella, walking hurriedly and so furiously angry that she did not recognise him, even to the extent of acknowledging his bow.

When Adam got back to Lesser Hill, he went to the coach-house where the box with the mongoose was kept, and took it with him, intending to finish at the Mound of Stone what he had begun the previous morning with regard to the extermination. He found that the snakes were even more easily attacked than on the previous day; no less than six were killed in the first half-hour. As no more appeared, he took it for granted that the morning's work was over, and went towards home. The mongoose had by this time become accustomed to him, and was willing to let himself be handled freely. Adam lifted him up and put him on his shoulder and walked on. Presently he saw a lady advancing towards him, and recognised Lady Arabella.

Hitherto the mongoose had been quiet, like a playful affectionate kitten; but when the two got close, Adam was horrified to see the mongoose, in a state of the wildest fury, with every hair standing on end, jump from his shoulder and run towards Lady Arabella. It looked so furious and so intent on attack that he called a warning.

"Look out – look out! The animal is furious and means to attack."

Lady Arabella looked more than ever disdainful and was passing on; the mongoose jumped at her in a furious attack. Adam rushed forward with his stick, the only weapon he had. But just as he got within striking distance, the lady drew out a revolver and shot the animal, breaking his backbone. Not satisfied with this, she poured shot after shot into him till the magazine was exhausted. There was no coolness or hauteur about her now; she seemed more furious even than the animal, her face transformed with hate, and as determined to kill as he had appeared to be. Adam, not knowing exactly what to do, lifted his hat in apology and hurried on to Lesser Hill.

CHAPTER VIII

SURVIVALS

AT BREAKFAST SIR NATHANIEL NOTICED that Adam was put out about something, but he said nothing. The lesson of silence is better remembered in age than in youth. When they were both in the study, where Sir Nathaniel followed him, Adam at once began to tell his companion of what had happened. Sir Nathaniel looked graver and graver as the narration proceeded, and when Adam had stopped he remained silent for several minutes, before speaking.

"This is very grave. I have not formed any opinion yet; but it seems to me at first impression that this is worse than anything I had expected."

"Why, sir?" said Adam. "Is the killing of a mongoose – no matter by whom – so serious a thing as all that?"

His companion smoked on quietly for quite another few minutes before he spoke.

"When I have properly thought it over I may moderate my opinion, but in the meantime it seems to me that there is something dreadful behind all this – something that may affect all our lives – that may mean the issue of life or death to any of us."

Adam sat up quickly.

"Do tell me, sir, what is in your mind – if, of course, you have no objection, or do not think it better to withhold it."

"I have no objection, Adam – in fact, if I had, I should have to overcome it. I fear there can be no more reserved thoughts between us."

"Indeed, sir, that sounds serious, worse than serious!"

"Adam, I greatly fear that the time has come for us – for you and me, at all events – to speak out plainly to one another. Does not there seem something very mysterious about this?"

"I have thought so, sir, all along. The only difficulty one has is what one is to think and where to begin."

"Let us begin with what you have told me. First take the conduct of the mongoose. He was quiet, even friendly and affectionate with you. He only attacked the snakes, which is, after all, his business in life."

"That is so!"

"Then we must try to find some reason why he attacked Lady Arabella."

"May it not be that a mongoose may have merely the instinct to attack, that nature does not allow or provide him with the fine reasoning powers to discriminate who he is to attack?"

"Of course that may be so. But, on the other hand, should we not satisfy ourselves why he does wish to attack anything? If for centuries, this particular animal is known to attack only one kind of other animal, are we not justified in assuming that when one of them attacks a hitherto unclassed animal, he recognises in that animal some quality which it has in common with the hereditary enemy?"

"That is a good argument, sir," Adam went on, "but a dangerous one. If we followed it out, it would lead us to believe that Lady Arabella is a snake."

"We must be sure, before going to such an end, that there is no point as yet unconsidered which would account for the unknown thing which puzzles us."

"In what way?"

"Well, suppose the instinct works on some physical basis – for instance, smell. If there were anything in recent juxtaposition to the attacked which would carry the scent, surely that would supply the missing cause."

"Of course!" Adam spoke with conviction.

"Now, from what you tell me, the negro had just come from the direction of Diana's Grove, carrying the dead snakes which the mongoose had killed the previous morning. Might not the scent have been carried that way?"

"Of course it might, and probably was. I never thought of that. Is there any possible way of guessing approximately how long a scent will remain? You see, this is a natural scent, and may derive from a place where it has been effective for thousands of years. Then, does a scent of any kind carry with it any form or quality of another kind, either good or evil? I ask you because one ancient name of the house lived in by the lady who was attacked by the mongoose was 'The Lair of the White Worm.' If any of these things be so, our difficulties have multiplied indefinitely. They may even change in kind. We may get into moral entanglements; before we know it, we may be in the midst of a struggle between good and evil."

Sir Nathaniel smiled gravely.

"With regard to the first question – so far as I know, there are no fixed periods for which a scent may be active – I think we may take it that that period does not run into thousands of years. As to whether any moral change accompanies a physical one, I can only say that I have met no proof of the fact. At the same time, we must remember that 'good' and 'evil' are terms so wide as to take in the whole scheme of creation, and all that is implied by them and by their mutual action and reaction. Generally, I would say that in the scheme of a First Cause anything is possible. So long as the inherent forces or tendencies of any one thing are veiled from us we must expect mystery."

"There is one other question on which I should like to ask your opinion. Suppose that there are any permanent forces appertaining to the past, what we may call 'survivals,' do these belong to good as well as to evil? For instance, if the scent of the primaeval monster can so remain in proportion to the original strength, can the same be true of things of good import?"

Sir Nathaniel thought for a while before he answered.

"We must be careful not to confuse the physical and the moral. I can see that already you have switched on the moral entirely, so perhaps we had better follow it up first. On the side of the moral, we have certain justification for belief in the utterances of revealed religion. For instance, 'the effectual fervent prayer of a righteous man availeth much' is altogether for good. We have nothing of a similar kind on the side of evil. But if we accept this dictum we need have no more fear of 'mysteries': these become thenceforth merely obstacles."

Adam suddenly changed to another phase of the subject.

"And now, sir, may I turn for a few minutes to purely practical things, or rather to matters of historical fact?"

Sir Nathaniel bowed acquiescence.

"We have already spoken of the history, so far as it is known, of some of the places round us – 'Castra Regis,' 'Diana's Grove,' and 'The Lair of the White Worm.' I would like to ask if there is anything not necessarily of evil import about any of the places?"

"Which?" asked Sir Nathaniel shrewdly.

"Well, for instance, this house and Mercy Farm?"

"Here we turn," said Sir Nathaniel, "to the other side, the light side of things. Let us take Mercy Farm first. When Augustine was sent by Pope Gregory to Christianise England, in the time of the Romans, he was received and protected by Ethelbert, King of Kent, whose wife, daughter of Charibert, King of Paris, was a Christian, and did much for Augustine. She founded a nunnery in memory of Columba, which was named *Sedes Misericordioe*, the House of Mercy, and, as the region was Mercian, the two names became involved. As Columba is the Latin for dove, the dove became a sort of signification of the nunnery. She seized on the idea and made the newly-founded nunnery a house of doves. Someone sent her a freshly-discovered dove, a sort of carrier, but which had in the white feathers of its head and neck the form of a religious cowl. The nunnery flourished for more than a century, when, in the time of Penda, who was the reactionary of heathendom, it fell into decay. In the meantime the doves, protected by religious feeling, had increased mightily, and were known in all Catholic communities. When King Offa ruled in Mercia, about a hundred and fifty years later, he restored Christianity, and under its protection the nunnery of St. Columba was restored and its doves flourished again. In process of time this religious house again fell into desuetude; but before it disappeared it had achieved a great name for good works, and in especial for the piety of its members. If deeds and prayers and hopes and earnest thinking leave anywhere any moral effect, Mercy Farm and all around it have almost the right to be considered holy ground."

"Thank you, sir," said Adam earnestly, and was silent. Sir Nathaniel understood.

After lunch that day, Adam casually asked Sir Nathaniel to come for a walk with him. The keen-witted old diplomatist guessed that there must be some motive behind the suggestion, and he at once agreed.

As soon as they were free from observation, Adam began.

"I am afraid, sir, that there is more going on in this neighbourhood than most people imagine. I was out this morning, and on the edge of the small wood, I came upon the body of a child by the roadside. At first, I thought she was dead, and while examining her, I noticed on her neck some marks that looked like those of teeth."

"Some wild dog, perhaps?" put in Sir Nathaniel.

"Possibly, sir, though I think not – but listen to the rest of my news. I glanced around, and to my surprise, I noticed something white moving among the trees. I placed the child down carefully, and followed, but I could not find any further traces. So I returned to the child and resumed my examination, and, to my delight, I discovered that she was still alive. I chafed her hands and gradually she revived, but to my disappointment she remembered nothing – except that something had crept up quietly from behind, and had gripped her round the throat. Then, apparently, she fainted."

"Gripped her round the throat! Then it cannot have been a dog."

"No, sir, that is my difficulty, and explains why I brought you out here, where we cannot possibly be overheard. You have noticed, of course, the peculiar sinuous way in which Lady Arabella moves – well, I feel certain that the white thing that I saw in the wood was the mistress of Diana's Grove!"

"Good God, boy, be careful what you say."

"Yes, sir, I fully realise the gravity of my accusation, but I feel convinced that the marks on the child's throat were human – and made by a woman."

Adam's companion remained silent for some time, deep in thought.

"Adam, my boy," he said at last, "this matter appears to me to be far more serious even than you think. It forces me to break confidence with my old friend, your uncle – but, in order to spare him, I must do so. For some time now, things have been happening in this district that have been worrying him dreadfully – several people have disappeared, without leaving the slightest trace; a dead child was found by the roadside, with no visible or ascertainable cause of death – sheep and other animals have been found in the fields, bleeding from open wounds. There have been other matters – many of them apparently trivial in themselves. Some sinister influence has been at work, and I admit that I have suspected Lady Arabella – that is why I questioned you so closely about the mongoose and its strange attack upon Lady Arabella. You will think it strange that I should suspect the mistress of Diana's Grove, a beautiful woman of aristocratic birth. Let me explain – the family seat is near my own place, Doom Tower, and at one time I knew the family well. When still a young girl, Lady Arabella wandered into a small wood near her home, and did not return. She was found unconscious and in a high fever – the doctor said that she had received a poisonous bite, and the girl being at a delicate and critical age, the result was serious – so much so that she was not expected to recover. A great London physician came down but could do nothing – indeed, he said that the girl would not survive the night. All hope had been abandoned, when, to everyone's surprise, Lady Arabella made a sudden and startling recovery. Within a couple of days she was going about as usual! But to the horror of her people, she developed a terrible craving for cruelty, maiming and injuring birds and small animals – even killing them. This was put down to a nervous disturbance due to her age, and it was hoped that her marriage to Captain March would put this right. However, it was not a happy marriage, and eventually her husband was found shot through the head. I have always suspected suicide, though no pistol was found near the body. He may have discovered something – God knows what! – so possibly Lady Arabella may herself have killed him. Putting together many small matters that have come to my knowledge, I have come to the conclusion that the foul White Worm obtained control of her body, just as her soul was leaving its earthly tenement – that would explain the sudden revival of energy, the strange and inexplicable craving for maiming and killing, as well as many other matters with which I need not trouble you now, Adam. As I said just now, God alone knows what poor Captain March discovered – it must have been something too ghastly for human endurance, if my theory is correct that the once beautiful human body of Lady Arabella is under the control of this ghastly White Worm."

Adam nodded.

"But what can we do, sir – it seems a most difficult problem."

"We can do nothing, my boy – that is the important part of it. It would be impossible to take action – all we can do is to keep careful watch, especially as regards Lady Arabella, and be ready to act, promptly and decisively, if the opportunity occurs."

Adam agreed, and the two men returned to Lesser Hill.

CHAPTER IX

SMELLING DEATH

ADAM SALTON, THOUGH HE talked little, did not let the grass grow under his feet in any matter which he had undertaken, or in which he was interested. He had agreed with Sir Nathaniel that they should not do anything with regard to the mystery of Lady Arabella's fear of the mongoose, but he steadily pursued his course in being *prepared* to act whenever the opportunity might come. He was in his own mind perpetually casting about for information or clues which might lead to possible lines of action. Baffled by the killing of the mongoose, he looked around for another line to follow. He was fascinated by the idea of there being a mysterious link between the woman and the animal, but he was already preparing a second string to his bow. His new idea was to use the faculties of Oolanga, so far as he could, in the service of discovery. His first move was to send Davenport to Liverpool to try to find the steward of the *West African*, who had told him about Oolanga, and if possible secure any further information, and then try to induce (by bribery or other means) the negro* to come to the Brow. So soon as he himself could have speech of the Voodoo-man he would be able to learn from him something useful. Davenport was successful in his missions, for he had to get another mongoose, and he was able to tell Adam that he had seen the steward, who told him much that he wanted to know, and had also arranged for Oolanga to come to Lesser Hill the following day. At this point Adam saw his way sufficiently clear to admit Davenport to some extent into his confidence. He had come to the conclusion that it would be better – certainly at first – not himself to appear in the matter, with which Davenport was fully competent to deal. It would be time for himself to take a personal part when matters had advanced a little further.

If what the African* said was in any wise true, the man had a rare gift which might be useful in the quest they were after. He could, as it were, "smell death." If any one was dead, if any one had died, or if a place had been used in connection with death, he seemed to know the broad fact by intuition. Adam made up his mind that to test this faculty with regard to several places would be his first task. Naturally he was anxious, and the time passed slowly. The only comfort was the arrival the next morning of a strong packing case, locked, from Ross, the key being in the custody of Davenport. In the case were two smaller boxes, both locked. One of them contained a mongoose to replace that killed by Lady Arabella; the other was the special mongoose which had already killed the king-cobra in Nepaul. When both the animals had been safely put under lock and key, he felt that he might breathe more freely. No one was allowed to know the secret of their existence in the house, except himself and Davenport. He arranged that Davenport should take Oolanga round the neighbourhood for a walk, stopping at each of the places which he designated. Having gone all along the Brow, he was to return the same way and induce him to touch on the same subjects in talking with Adam, who was to meet them as if by chance at the farthest part – that beyond Mercy Farm.

The incidents of the day proved much as Adam expected. At Mercy Farm, at Diana's Grove, at Castra Regis, and a few other spots, the negro stopped and, opening his wide nostrils as if to sniff boldly, said that he smelled death. It was not always in the same form. At Mercy Farm he said there were many small deaths. At Diana's Grove his bearing was different. There was a distinct sense of enjoyment about him, especially when he spoke of many great deaths. Here, too, he sniffed in a strange way, like a bloodhound at check, and looked puzzled. He said no word in either praise or disparagement, but in the centre of the Grove, where, hidden amongst ancient oak stumps, was a block of granite slightly hollowed on the top, he bent low and placed his forehead on the ground. This was the only place where he showed distinct reverence. At the Castle, though he spoke of much death, he showed no sign of respect.

There was evidently something about Diana's Grove which both interested and baffled him. Before leaving, he moved all over the place unsatisfied, and in one spot, close to the edge of the Brow, where there was a deep hollow, he appeared to be afraid. After returning several times to this place, he suddenly turned and ran in a panic of fear to the higher ground, crossing as he did so the outcropping rock. Then he seemed to breathe more freely, and recovered some of his jaunty impudence.

All this seemed to satisfy Adam's expectations. He went back to Lesser Hill with a serene and settled calm upon him. Sir Nathaniel followed him into his study.

"By the way, I forgot to ask you details about one thing. When that extraordinary staring episode of Mr. Caswall went on, how did Lilla take it – how did she bear herself?"

"She looked frightened, and trembled just as I have seen a pigeon with a hawk, or a bird with a serpent."

"Thanks. It is just as I expected. There have been circumstances in the Caswall family which lead one to believe that they have had from the earliest times some extraordinary mesmeric or hypnotic faculty. Indeed, a skilled eye could read so much in their physiognomy. That shot of yours, whether by instinct or intention, of the hawk and the pigeon was peculiarly apposite. I think we may settle on that as a fixed trait to be accepted throughout our investigation."

When dusk had fallen, Adam took the new mongoose – not the one from Nepaul – and, carrying the box slung over his shoulder, strolled towards Diana's Grove. Close to the gateway he met Lady Arabella, clad as usual in tightly fitting white, which showed off her slim figure.

To his intense astonishment the mongoose allowed her to pet him, take him up in her arms and fondle him. As she was going in his direction, they walked on together.

Round the roadway between the entrances of Diana's Grove and Lesser Hill were many trees, with not much foliage except at the top. In the dusk this place was shadowy, and the view was hampered by the clustering trunks. In the uncertain, tremulous light which fell through the tree-tops, it was hard to distinguish anything clearly, and at last, somehow, he lost sight of her altogether, and turned back on his track to find her. Presently he came across her close to her own gate. She was leaning over the paling of split oak branches which formed the paling of the avenue. He could not see the mongoose, so he asked her where it had gone.

"He slipt out of my arms while I was petting him," she answered, "and disappeared under the hedges."

They found him at a place where the avenue widened so as to let carriages pass each other. The little creature seemed quite changed. He had been ebulliently active; now he was dull and spiritless – seemed to be dazed. He allowed himself to be lifted by either of the pair; but when he was alone with Lady Arabella he kept looking round him in a strange way, as though trying to escape. When they had come out on the roadway Adam held the mongoose tight to him, and, lifting his hat to his companion, moved quickly towards Lesser Hill; he and Lady Arabella lost sight of each other in the thickening gloom.

When Adam got home, he put the mongoose in his box, and locked the door of the room. The other mongoose – the one from Nepaul – was safely locked in his own box, but he lay quiet and did not stir. When he got to his study Sir Nathaniel came in, shutting the door behind him.

"I have come," he said, "while we have an opportunity of being alone, to tell you something of the Caswall family which I think will interest you. There is, or used to be, a belief in this part of the world that the Caswall family had some strange power of making the wills of other persons subservient to their own. There are many allusions to the subject in memoirs and other unimportant works, but I only know of one where the subject is spoken of definitely. It is *Mercia and its Worthies*, written by Ezra Toms more than a hundred years ago. The author goes into the question of the close association of the then Edgar Caswall with Mesmer in Paris. He speaks of Caswall being a pupil and the fellow worker of Mesmer, and states that though, when the latter left France, he took away with him a vast quantity of philosophical and electric instruments, he was never known to use them again. He once made it known to a friend that he had given them to his old pupil. The term he used was odd, for it was 'bequeathed,' but no such bequest of Mesmer was ever made known. At any rate the instruments were missing, and never turned up."

A servant came into the room to tell Adam that there was some strange noise coming from the locked room into which he had gone when he came in. He hurried off to the place at once, Sir Nathaniel going with him. Having locked the door behind them, Adam opened the packing-case where the boxes of the two mongooses were locked up. There was no sound from one of them, but from the other a queer restless struggling. Having opened both boxes, he found that the noise was from the Nepaul animal, which, however, became quiet at once. In the other box the new mongoose lay dead, with every appearance of having been strangled!

CHAPTER X

THE KITE

ON THE FOLLOWING DAY, A little after four o'clock, Adam set out for Mercy.

He was home just as the clocks were striking six. He was pale and upset, but otherwise looked strong and alert. The old man summed up his appearance and manner thus: "Braced up for battle."

"Now!" said Sir Nathaniel, and settled down to listen, looking at Adam steadily and listening attentively that he might miss nothing – even the inflection of a word.

"I found Lilla and Mimi at home. Watford had been detained by business on the farm. Miss Watford received me as kindly as before; Mimi, too, seemed glad to see me. Mr. Caswall came so soon after I arrived, that he, or someone on his behalf, must have been watching for me. He was followed closely by the negro, who was puffing hard as if he had been running – so it was probably he

who watched. Mr. Caswall was very cool and collected, but there
was a more than usually iron look about his face that I did not
like. However, we got on very well. He talked pleasantly on all
sorts of questions. The negro* waited a while and then disappeared as on the other occasion. Mr. Caswall's eyes were as usual
fixed on Lilla. True, they seemed to be very deep and earnest, but
there was no offence in them. Had it not been for the drawing
down of the brows and the stern set of the jaws, I should not at
first have noticed anything. But the stare, when presently it began,
increased in intensity. I could see that Lilla began to suffer from
nervousness, as on the first occasion; but she carried herself
bravely. However, the more nervous she grew, the harder Mr. Caswall stared. It was evident to me that he had come prepared for
some sort of mesmeric or hypnotic battle. After a while he began
to throw glances round him and then raised his hand, without
letting either Lilla or Mimi see the action. It was evidently intended to give some sign to the negro, for he came, in his usual
stealthy way, quietly in by the hall door, which was open. Then
Mr. Caswall's efforts at staring became intensified, and poor Lilla's
nervousness grew greater. Mimi, seeing that her cousin was distressed, came close to her, as if to comfort or strengthen her with
the consciousness of her presence. This evidently made a difficulty for Mr. Caswall, for his efforts, without appearing to get fee-
bler, seemed less effective. This continued for a little while, to the
gain of both Lilla and Mimi. Then there was a diversion. Without
word or apology the door opened, and Lady Arabella March entered the room. I had seen her coming through the great window.
Without a word she crossed the room and stood beside Mr. Caswall. It really was very like a fight of a peculiar kind; and the
longer it was sustained the more earnest – the fiercer – it grew.
That combination of forces – the over-lord, the white woman,
and the black man – would have cost some – probably all of them
– their lives in the Southern States of America. To us it was simply horrible. But all that you can understand. This time, to go on
in sporting phrase, it was understood by all to be a 'fight to a finish,' and the mixed group did not slacken a moment or relax their
efforts. On Lilla the strain began to tell disastrously. She grew pale
– a patchy pallor, which meant that her nerves were out of order.
She trembled like an aspen, and though she struggled bravely, I
noticed that her legs would hardly support her. A dozen times she
seemed about to collapse in a faint, but each time, on catching
sight of Mimi's eyes, she made a fresh struggle and pulled
through.

"By now Mr. Caswall's face had lost its appearance of passivity.
His eyes glowed with a fiery light. He was still the old Roman in
inflexibility of purpose; but grafted on to the Roman was a new

Berserker fury. His companions in the baleful work seemed to have taken on something of his feeling. Lady Arabella looked like a soulless, pitiless being, not human, unless it revived old legends of transformed human beings who had lost their humanity in some transformation or in the sweep of natural savagery. As for the negro – well, I can only say that it was solely due to the self-restraint which you impressed on me that I did not wipe him out as he stood – without warning, without fair play – without a single one of the graces of life and death. Lilla was silent in the helpless concentration of deadly fear; Mimi was all resolve and self-forgetfulness, so intent on the soul-struggle in which she was engaged that there was no possibility of any other thought. As for myself, the bonds of will which held me inactive seemed like bands of steel which numbed all my faculties, except sight and hearing. We seemed fixed in an *impasse*. Something must happen, though the power of guessing was inactive. As in a dream, I saw Mimi's hand move restlessly, as if groping for something. Mechanically it touched that of Lilla, and in that instant she was transformed. It was as if youth and strength entered afresh into something already dead to sensibility and intention. As if by inspiration, she grasped the other's band with a force which blenched the knuckles. Her face suddenly flamed, as if some divine light shone through it. Her form expanded till it stood out majestically. Lifting her right hand, she stepped forward towards Caswall, and with a bold sweep of her arm seemed to drive some strange force towards him. Again and again was the gesture repeated, the man falling back from her at each movement. Towards the door he retreated, she following. There was a sound as of the cooing sob of doves, which seemed to multiply and intensify with each second. The sound from the unseen source rose and rose as he retreated, till finally it swelled out in a triumphant peal, as she with a fierce sweep of her arm, seemed to hurl something at her foe, and he, moving his hands blindly before his face, appeared to be swept through the doorway and out into the open sunlight.

"All at once my own faculties were fully restored; I could see and hear everything, and be fully conscious of what was going on. Even the figures of the baleful group were there, though dimly seen as through a veil – a shadowy veil. I saw Lilla sink down in a swoon, and Mimi throw up her arms in a gesture of triumph. As I saw her through the great window, the sunshine flooded the landscape, which, however, was momentarily becoming eclipsed by an onrush of a myriad birds."

By the next morning, daylight showed the actual danger which threatened. From every part of the eastern counties reports were received concerning the enormous immigration of birds. Experts were sending – on their own account, on behalf of learned societies, and through local and imperial governing bodies – reports dealing with the matter, and suggesting remedies.

The reports closer to home were even more disturbing. All day long it would seem that the birds were coming thicker from all quarters. Doubtless many were going as well as coming, but the mass seemed never to get less. Each bird seemed to sound some note of fear or anger or seeking, and the whirring of wings never ceased nor lessened. The air was full of a muttered throb. No window or barrier could shut out the sound, till the ears of any listener became dulled by the ceaseless murmur. So monotonous it was, so cheerless, so disheartening, so melancholy, that all longed, but in vain, for any variety, no matter how terrible it might be.

The second morning the reports from all the districts round were more alarming than ever. Farmers began to dread the coming of winter as they saw the dwindling of the timely fruitfulness of the earth. And as yet it was only a warning of evil, not the evil accomplished; the ground began to look bare whenever some passing sound temporarily frightened the birds.

Edgar Caswall tortured his brain for a long time unavailingly, to think of some means of getting rid of what he, as well as his neighbours, had come to regard as a plague of birds. At last he recalled a circumstance which promised a solution of the difficulty. The experience was of some years ago in China, far up-country, towards the head-waters of the Yang-tze-kiang, where the smaller tributaries spread out in a sort of natural irrigation scheme to supply the wilderness of paddy-fields. It was at the time of the ripening rice, and the myriads of birds which came to feed on the coming crop was a serious menace, not only to the district, but to the country at large. The farmers, who were more or less afflicted with the same trouble every season, knew how to deal with it. They made a vast kite, which they caused to be flown over the centre spot of the incursion. The kite was shaped like a great hawk; and the moment it rose into the air the birds began to cower and seek protection – and then to disappear. So long as that kite was flying overhead the birds lay low and the crop was saved. Accordingly Caswall ordered his men to construct an immense kite, adhering as well as they could to the lines of a hawk. Then he and his men, with a sufficiency of cord, began to fly it high overhead. The experience of China was repeated. The moment the kite rose, the birds hid or sought shelter. The following morning, the kite was still flying high, no bird was to be seen as far as the eye could reach from Castra Regis. But there followed in turn what proved even a worse evil. All the birds were cowed; their sounds stopped. Neither song nor chirp was heard – silence seemed to have taken the place of the normal voices of bird life.

But that was not all. The silence spread to all animals.

The fear and restraint which brooded amongst the denizens of the air began to affect all life. Not only did the birds cease song or chirp, but the lowing of the cattle ceased in the fields and the varied sounds of life died away. In place of these things was only a soundless gloom, more dreadful, more disheartening, more soul-killing than any concourse of sounds, no matter how full of fear and dread. Pious individuals put up constant prayers for relief from the intolerable solitude. After a little there were signs of universal depression which those who ran might read. One and all, the faces of men and women seemed bereft of vitality, of interest, of thought, and, most of all, of hope. Men seemed to have lost the power of expression of their thoughts. The soundless air seemed to have the same effect as the universal darkness when men gnawed their tongues with pain.

From this infliction of silence there was no relief. Everything was affected; gloom was the predominant note. Joy appeared to have passed away as a factor of life, and this creative impulse had nothing to take its place. That giant spot in high air was a plague of evil influence. It seemed like a new misanthropic belief which had fallen on human beings, carrying with it the negation of all hope.

After a few days, men began to grow desperate; their very words as well as their senses seemed to be in chains. Edgar Caswall again tortured his brain to find any antidote or palliative of this greater evil than before. He would gladly have destroyed the kite, or caused its flying to cease; but the instant it was pulled down, the birds rose up in even greater numbers; all those who depended in any way on agriculture sent pitiful protests to Castra Regis.

It was strange indeed what influence that weird kite seemed to exercise. Even human beings were affected by it, as if both it and they were realities. As for the people at Mercy Farm, it was like a taste of actual death. Lilla felt it most. If she had been indeed a real dove, with a real kite hanging over her in the air, she could not have been more frightened or more affected by the terror this created.

Of course, some of those already drawn into the vortex noticed the effect on individuals. Those who were interested took care to compare their information. Strangely enough, as it seemed to the others, the person who took the ghastly silence least to heart was the negro. By nature he was not sensitive to, or afflicted by, nerves. This alone would not have produced the seeming indifference, so they set their minds to discover the real cause. Adam came quickly to the conclusion that there was for him some compensation that the others did not share; and he soon believed that

that compensation was in one form or another the enjoyment of the sufferings of others. Thus the black had a never-failing source of amusement.

Lady Arabella's cold nature rendered her immune to anything in the way of pain or trouble concerning others. Edgar Caswall was far too haughty a person, and too stern of nature, to concern himself about poor or helpless people, much less the lower order of mere animals. Mr. Watford, Mr. Salton, and Sir Nathaniel were all concerned in the issue, partly from kindness of heart – for none of them could see suffering, even of wild birds, unmoved – and partly on account of their property, which had to be protected, or ruin would stare them in the face before long.

Lilla suffered acutely. As time went on, her face became pinched, and her eyes dull with watching and crying. Mimi suffered too on account of her cousin's suffering. But as she could do nothing, she resolutely made up her mind to self-restraint and patience. Adam's frequent visits comforted her.

CHAPTER XI
MESMER'S CHEST

AFTER A COUPLE OF WEEKS HAD passed, the kite seemed to give Edgar Caswall a new zest for life. He was never tired of looking at its movements. He had a comfortable armchair put out on the tower, wherein he sat sometimes all day long, watching as though the kite was a new toy and he a child lately come into possession of it. He did not seem to have lost interest in Lilla, for he still paid an occasional visit at Mercy Farm.

Indeed, his feeling towards her, whatever it had been at first, had now so far changed that it had become a distinct affection of a purely animal kind. Indeed, it seemed as though the man's nature had become corrupted, and that all the baser and more selfish and more reckless qualities had become more conspicuous. There was not so much sternness apparent in his nature, because there was less self-restraint. Determination had become indifference.

The visible change in Edgar was that he grew morbid, sad, silent; the neighbours thought he was going mad. He became absorbed in the kite, and watched it not only by day, but often all night long. It became an obsession to him.

Caswall took a personal interest in the keeping of the great kite flying. He had a vast coil of cord efficient for the purpose, which worked on a roller fixed on the parapet of the tower. There was a winch for the pulling in of the slack; the outgoing line being controlled by a racket. There was invariably one man at least, day and night, on the tower to attend to it. At such an elevation there was always a strong wind, and at times the kite rose to an enormous height, as well as travelling for great distances laterally. In fact, the kite became, in a short time, one of the curiosities of Castra Regis and all around it. Edgar began to attribute to it, in his own mind, almost human qualities. It became to him a separate entity, with a mind and a soul of its own. Being idle-handed all day, he began to apply to what he considered the service of the kite some of his spare time, and found a new pleasure – a new object in life – in the old schoolboy game of sending up "runners" to the kite. The way this is done is to get round pieces of paper so cut that there is a hole in the centre, through which the string of the kite passes. The natural action of the wind-pressure takes the paper along the string, and so up to the kite itself, no matter how high or how far it may have gone.

In the early days of this amusement Edgar Caswall spent hours. Hundreds of such messengers flew along the string, until soon he bethought him of writing messages on these papers so that he could make known his ideas to the kite. It may be that his brain gave way under the opportunities given by his illusion of the entity of the toy and its power of separate thought. From sending messages he came to making direct speech to the kite – without, however, ceasing to send the runners. Doubtless, the height of the tower, seated as it was on the hill-top, the rushing of the ceaseless wind, the hypnotic effect of the lofty altitude of the speck in the sky at which he gazed, and the rushing of the paper messengers up the string till sight of them was lost in distance, all helped to further affect his brain, undoubtedly giving way under the strain of beliefs and circumstances which were at once stimulating to the imagination, occupative of his mind, and absorbing.

The next step of intellectual decline was to bring to bear on the main idea of the conscious identity of the kite all sorts of subjects which had imaginative force or tendency of their own. He had, in Castra Regis, a large collection of curious and interesting things formed in the past by his forebears, of similar tastes to his own. There were all sorts of strange anthropological specimens, both old and new, which had been collected through various travels in strange places: ancient Egyptian relics from tombs and mummies; curios from Australia, New Zealand, and the South Seas; idols and images – from Tartar ikons to ancient Egyptian, Persian, and Indian objects of worship; objects of death and torture of American Indians; and, above all, a vast collection of lethal weapons of every kind and from every place – Chinese "high pinders," double knives, Afghan double-edged scimitars made to cut a body in two, heavy knives from all the Eastern countries, ghost daggers from Thibet, the terrible kukri of the Ghourka and other hill tribes of India, assassins' weapons from Italy and Spain, even the knife which was formerly carried by the slave-drivers of the Mississippi region. Death and pain of every kind were fully represented in that gruesome collection.

That it had a fascination for Oolanga goes without saying. He was never tired of visiting the museum in the tower, and spent endless hours in inspecting the exhibits, till he was thoroughly familiar with every detail of all of them. He asked permission to clean and polish and sharpen them – a favour which was readily granted. In addition to the above objects, there were many things of a kind to awaken human fear. Stuffed serpents of the most objectionable and horrid kind; giant insects from the tropics, fearsome in every detail; fishes and crustaceans covered with weird spikes; dried octopuses of great size. Other things, too, there were, not less deadly though seemingly innocuous – dried fungi, traps intended for birds, beasts, fishes, reptiles, and insects; machines which could produce pain of any kind and degree, and the only mercy of which was the power of producing speedy death.

Caswall, who had never before seen any of these things, except those which he had collected himself, found a constant amusement and interest in them. He studied them, their uses, their mechanism – where there was such – and their places of origin, until he had an ample and real knowledge of all concerning them. Many were secret and intricate, but he never rested till he found out all the secrets. When once he had become interested in strange objects, and the way to use them, he began to explore various likely places for similar finds. He began to inquire of his household where strange lumber was kept. Several of the men spoke of old Simon Chester as one who knew everything in and about the house. Accordingly, he sent for the old man, who came at once. He was very old, nearly ninety years of age, and very infirm. He had been born in the Castle, and had served its succession of masters – present or absent – ever since. When Edgar began to question him on the subject regarding which he had sent for him, old Simon exhibited much perturbation. In fact, he became so frightened that his master, fully believing that he was concealing something, ordered him to tell at once what remained unseen, and where it was hidden away. Face to face with discovery of his secret, the old man, in a pitiable state of concern, spoke out even more fully than Mr. Caswall had expected.

"Indeed, indeed, sir, everything is here in the tower that has ever been put away in my time except – except – " here he began to shake and tremble it – "except the chest which Mr. Edgar – he who was Mr. Edgar when I first took service – brought back from France, after he had been with Dr. Mesmer. The trunk has been kept in my room for safety; but I shall send it down here now."

"What is in it?" asked Edgar sharply.

"That I do not know. Moreover, it is a peculiar trunk, without any visible means of opening."

"Is there no lock?"

"I suppose so, sir; but I do not know. There is no keyhole."

"Send it here; and then come to me yourself."

The trunk, a heavy one with steel bands round it, but no lock or keyhole, was carried in by two men. Shortly afterwards old Simon attended his master. When he came into the room, Mr. Caswall himself went and closed the door; then he asked:

"How do you open it?"

"I do not know, sir."

"Do you mean to say that you never opened it?"

"Most certainly I say so, your honour. How could I? It was entrusted to me with the other things by my master. To open it would have been a breach of trust."

Caswall sneered.

"Quite remarkable! Leave it with me. Close the door behind you. Stay – did no one ever tell you about it – say anything regarding it – make any remark?"

Old Simon turned pale, and put his trembling hands together.

"Oh, sir, I entreat you not to touch it. That trunk probably contains secrets which Dr. Mesmer told my master. Told them to his ruin!"

"How do you mean? What ruin?"

"Sir, he it was who, men said, sold his soul to the Evil One; I had thought that that time and the evil of it had all passed away."

"That will do. Go away; but remain in your own room, or within call. I may want you."

The old man bowed deeply and went out trembling, but without speaking a word.

CHAPTER XII

THE CHEST OPENED

LEFT ALONE IN THE TURRET-ROOM, Edgar Caswall carefully locked the door and hung a handkerchief over the keyhole. Next, he inspected the windows, and saw that they were not overlooked from any angle of the main building. Then he carefully examined the trunk, going over it with a magnifying glass. He found it intact: the steel bands were flawless; the whole trunk was compact. After sitting opposite to it for some time, and the shades of evening beginning to melt into darkness, he gave up the task and went to his bedroom, after locking the door of the turret-room behind him and taking away the key.

He woke in the morning at daylight, and resumed his patient but unavailing study of the metal trunk. This he continued during the whole day with the same result – humiliating disappointment, which overwrought his nerves and made his head ache. The result of the long strain was seen later in the afternoon, when he sat locked within the turret-room before the still baffling trunk, distrait, listless and yet agitated, sunk in a settled gloom. As the dusk was falling he told the steward to send him two men, strong ones. These he ordered to take the trunk to his bedroom. In that room he then sat on into the night, without pausing even to take any food. His mind was in a whirl, a fever of excitement. The result was that when, late in the night, he locked himself in his room his brain was full of odd fancies; he was on the high road to mental disturbance. He lay down on his bed in the dark, still brooding over the mystery of the closed trunk.

Gradually he yielded to the influences of silence and darkness. After lying there quietly for some time, his mind became active again. But this time there were round him no disturbing influences; his brain was active and able to work freely and to deal with memory. A thousand forgotten – or only half-known – incidents, fragments of conversations or theories long ago guessed at and long forgotten, crowded on his mind. He seemed to hear again around him the legions of whirring wings to which he had been so lately accustomed. Even to himself he knew that that was an effort of imagination founded on imperfect memory. But he was content that imagination should work, for out of it might come some solution of the mystery which surrounded him. And in this frame of mind, sleep made another and more successful essay. This time he enjoyed peaceful slumber, restful alike to his wearied body and his overwrought brain.

In his sleep he arose, and, as if in obedience to some influence beyond and greater than himself, lifted the great trunk and set it on a strong table at one side of the room, from which he had previously removed a quantity of books. To do this, he had to use an amount of strength which was, he knew, far beyond him in his normal state. As it was, it seemed easy enough; everything yielded before his touch. Then he became conscious that somehow – how, he never could remember – the chest was open. He unlocked his door, and, taking the chest on his shoulder, carried it up to the turret-room, the door of which also he unlocked. Even at the time he was amazed at his own strength, and wondered whence it had come. His mind, lost in conjecture, was too far off to realise more immediate things. He knew that the chest was enormously heavy. He seemed, in a sort of vision which lit up the absolute blackness around, to see the two sturdy servant men staggering under its great weight. He locked himself again in the turret-room, and laid the opened chest on a table, and in the darkness began to unpack it, laying out the contents, which were mainly of metal and glass – great pieces in strange forms – on another table. He was conscious of being still asleep, and of acting rather in obedience to some unseen and unknown command than in accordance with any reasonable plan, to be followed by results which he understood. This phase completed, he proceeded to arrange in order the component parts of some large instruments, formed mostly of glass. His fingers seemed to have acquired a new and exquisite subtlety and even a volition of their own. Then weariness of brain came upon him; his head sank down on his breast, and little by little everything became wrapped in gloom.

He awoke in the early morning in his bedroom, and looked around him, now clear-headed, in amazement. In its usual place on the strong table stood the great steel-hooped chest without lock or key. But it was now locked. He arose quietly and stole to the turret-room. There everything was as it had been on the previous evening. He looked out of the window where high in air flew, as usual, the giant kite. He unlocked the wicket gate of the turret stair and went out on the roof. Close to him was the great coil of cord on its reel. It was humming in the morning breeze, and when he touched the string it sent a quick thrill through hand and arm. There was no sign anywhere that there had been any disturbance or displacement of anything during the night.

Utterly bewildered, he sat down in his room to think. Now for the first time he *felt* that he was asleep and dreaming. Presently he fell asleep again, and slept for a long time. He awoke hungry and made a hearty meal. Then towards evening, having locked himself in, he fell asleep again. When he woke he was in darkness, and was quite at sea as to his whereabouts. He began feeling about the dark room, and was recalled to the consequences of his position by the breaking of a large piece of glass. Having obtained a light, he discovered this to be a glass wheel, part of an elaborate piece of mechanism which he must in his sleep have taken from the chest, which was now opened. He had once again opened it whilst asleep, but he had no recollection of the circumstances.

Caswall came to the conclusion that there had been some sort of dual action of his mind, which might lead to some catastrophe or some discovery of his secret plans; so he resolved to forgo for a while the pleasure of making discoveries regarding the chest. To this end, he applied himself to quite another matter – an investigation of the other treasures and rare objects in his collections. He went amongst them in simple, idle curiosity, his main object being to discover some strange item which he might use for experiment with the kite. He had already resolved to try some runners other than those made of paper. He had a vague idea that with such a force as the great kite straining at its leash, this might be used to lift to the altitude of the kite itself heavier articles. His first experiment with articles of little but increasing weight was eminently successful. So he added by degrees more and more weight, until he found out that the lifting power of the kite was considerable. He then determined to take a step further, and send to the kite some of the articles which lay in the steel-hooped chest. The last time he had opened it in sleep, it had not been shut again, and he had inserted a wedge so that he could open it at will. He made examination of the contents, but came to the conclusion that the glass objects were unsuitable. They were too light for testing weight, and they were so frail as to be dangerous to send to such a height.

So he looked around for something more solid with which to experiment. His eye caught sight of an object which at once attracted him. This was a small copy of one of the ancient Egyptian gods – that of Bes, who represented the destructive power of nature. It was so bizarre and mysterious as to commend itself to his mad humour. In lifting it from the cabinet, he was struck by its great weight in proportion to its size. He made accurate examination of it by the aid of some instruments, and came to the conclusion that it was carved from a lump of lodestone. He remembered that he had read somewhere of an ancient Egyptian god cut from a similar substance, and, thinking it over, he came to the conclusion that he must have read it in Sir Thomas Brown's *Popular Errors*, a book of the seventeenth century. He got the book from the library, and looked out the passage:

"A great example we have from the observation of our learned friend Mr. Graves, in an Ægyptian idol cut out of Loadstone and found among the Mummies; which still retains its attraction, though probably taken out of the mine about two thousand years ago."

The strangeness of the figure, and its being so close akin to his own nature, attracted him. He made from thin wood a large circular runner, and in front of it placed the weighty god, sending it up to the flying kite along the throbbing cord.

CHAPTER XIII

OOLANGA'S HALLUCINATIONS

DURING THE LAST FEW DAYS Lady Arabella had been getting exceedingly impatient. Her debts, always pressing, were growing to an embarrassing amount. The only hope she had of comfort in life was a good marriage; but the good marriage on which she had fixed her eye did not seem to move quickly enough – indeed, it did not seem to move at all – in the right direction. Edgar Caswall was not an ardent wooer. From the very first he seemed *difficile*, but he had been keeping to his own room ever since his struggle with Mimi Watford. On that occasion Lady Arabella had shown him in an unmistakable way what her feelings were; indeed, she had made it known to him, in a more overt way than pride should allow, that she wished to help and support him. The moment when she had gone across the room to stand beside him in his mesmeric struggle, had been the very limit of her voluntary action. It was quite bitter enough, she felt, that he did not come to her, but now that she had made that advance, she felt that any withdrawal on his part would, to a woman of her class, be nothing less than a flaming insult. Had she not classed herself with his nigger servant, an unreformed savage? Had she not shown her preference for him at the festival of his home-coming? Had she not. . . Lady Arabella was cold-blooded, and she was prepared to go through all that might be necessary of indifference, and even insult, to become chatelaine of Castra Regis. In the meantime, she would show no hurry – she must wait. She might, in an unostentatious way, come to him again. She knew him now, and could make a keen guess at his desires with regard to Lilla Watford. With that secret in her possession, she could bring pressure to bear on Caswall which would make it no easy matter for him to evade her. The great difficulty was how to get near him. He was shut up within his Castle, and guarded by a defence of convention which she could not pass without danger of ill repute to herself. Over this question she thought and thought for days and nights. At last she decided that the only way would be to go to him openly at Castra Regis. Her rank and position would make such a thing possible, if carefully done. She could explain matters afterwards if necessary. Then when they were alone, she would use her arts and her experience to make him commit himself. After all, he was only a man, with a man's dislike of difficult or awkward situations. She felt quite sufficient confidence in her own womanhood to carry her through any difficulty which might arise.

From Diana's Grove she heard each day the luncheon-gong from Castra Regis sound, and knew the hour when the servants would be in the back of the house. She would enter the house at that hour, and, pretending that she could not make anyone hear her, would seek him in his own rooms. The tower was, she knew, away from all the usual sounds of the house, and moreover she knew that the servants had strict orders not to interrupt him when he was in the turret chamber. She had found out, partly by the aid of an opera-glass and partly by judicious questioning, that several times lately a heavy chest had been carried to and from his room, and that it rested in the room each night. She was, therefore, confident that he had some important work on hand which would keep him busy for long spells.

Meanwhile, another member of the household at Castra Regis had schemes which he thought were working to fruition. A man in the position of a servant has plenty of opportunity of watching his betters and forming opinions regarding them. Oolanga was in his way a clever, unscrupulous rogue, and he felt that with things moving round him in this great household there should be opportunities of self-advancement. Being unscrupulous and stealthy – and a savage – he looked to dishonest means. He saw plainly enough that Lady Arabella was making a dead set at his master, and he was watchful of the slightest sign of anything which might enhance this knowledge. Like the other men in the house, he knew of the carrying to and fro of the great chest, and had got it into his head that the care exercised in its porterage indicated that it was full of treasure. He was for ever lurking around the turret-rooms on the chance of making some useful discovery. But he was as cautious as he was stealthy, and took care that no one else watched him.

It was thus that the negro became aware of Lady Arabella's venture into the house, as she thought, unseen. He took more care than ever, since he was watching another, that the positions were not reversed. More than ever he kept his eyes and ears open and his mouth shut. Seeing Lady Arabella gliding up the stairs towards his master's room, he took it for granted that she was there for no good, and doubled his watching intentness and caution.

Oolanga was disappointed, but he dared not exhibit any feeling lest it should betray that he was hiding. Therefore he slunk downstairs again noiselessly, and waited for a more favourable opportunity of furthering his plans. It must be borne in mind that he thought that the heavy trunk was full of valuables, and that he believed that Lady Arabella had come to try to steal it. His purpose of using for his own advantage the combination of these two ideas was seen later in the day. Oolanga secretly followed her home. He was an expert at this game, and succeeded admirably on this occasion. He watched her enter the private gate of Diana's Grove, and then, taking a roundabout course and keeping out of her sight, he at last overtook her in a thick part of the Grove where no one could see the meeting.

Lady Arabella was much surprised. She had not seen the negro for several days, and had almost forgotten his existence. Oolanga would have been startled had he known and been capable of understanding the real value placed on him, his beauty, his worthiness, by other persons, and compared it with the value in these matters in which he held himself. Doubtless Oolanga had his dreams like other men. In such cases he saw himself as a young sun-god, as beautiful as the eye of dusky or even white womanhood had ever dwelt upon. He would have been filled with all noble and captivating qualities – or those regarded as such in West Africa. Women would have loved him, and would have told him so in the overt and fervid manner usual in affairs of the heart in the shadowy depths of the forest of the Gold Coast.

Oolanga came close behind Lady Arabella, and in a hushed voice, suitable to the importance of his task, and in deference to the respect he had for her and the place, began to unfold the story of his love. Lady Arabella was not usually a humorous person, but no man or woman of the white race could have checked the laughter which rose spontaneously to her lips. The circumstances were too grotesque, the contrast too violent, for subdued mirth. The man a debased specimen of one of the most primitive races of the earth, and of an ugliness which was simply devilish; the woman of high degree, beautiful, accomplished. She thought that her first moment's consideration of the outrage – it was nothing less in her eyes – had given her the full material for thought. But every instant after threw new and varied lights on the affront. Her indignation was too great for passion; only irony or satire would meet the situation. Her cold, cruel nature helped, and she did not shrink to subject this ignorant savage to the merciless fire-lash of her scorn.

Oolanga was dimly conscious that he was being flouted; but his anger was no less keen because of the measure of his ignorance. So he gave way to it, as does a tortured beast. He ground his great teeth together, raved, stamped, and swore in barbarous tongues and with barbarous imagery. Even Lady Arabella felt that it was well she was within reach of help, or he might have offered her brutal violence – even have killed her.

"Am I to understand," she said with cold disdain, so much more effective to wound than hot passion, "that you are offering me your love? Your – love?"

For reply he nodded his head. The scorn of her voice, in a sort of baleful hiss, sounded – and felt – like the lash of a whip.

"And you dared! You – a savage – a slave – the basest thing in the world of vermin! Take care! I don't value your worthless life more than I do that of a rat or a spider. Don't let me ever see your hideous face here again, or I shall rid the earth of you."

As she was speaking, she had taken out her revolver and was pointing it at him. In the immediate presence of death his impudence forsook him, and he made a weak effort to justify himself. His speech was short, consisting of single words. To Lady Arabella it sounded mere gibberish, but it was in his own dialect, and meant love, marriage, wife. From the intonation of the words, she guessed, with her woman's quick intuition, at their meaning; but she quite failed to follow, when, becoming more pressing, he continued to urge his suit in a mixture of the grossest animal passion and ridiculous threats. He warned her that he knew she had tried to steal his master's treasure, and that he had caught her in the act. But if she would be his, he would share the treasure with her, and they could live in luxury in the African forests. But if she refused, he would tell his master, who would flog and torture her and then give her to the police, who would kill her.

CHAPTER XIV

BATTLE RENEWED

THE CONSEQUENCES OF THAT meeting in the dusk of Diana's Grove were acute and far-reaching, and not only to the two engaged in it. From Oolanga, this might have been expected by anyone who knew the character of the tropical African savage. To such, there are two passions that are inexhaustible and insatiable – vanity and that which they are pleased to call love. Oolanga left the Grove with an absorbing hatred in his heart. His lust and greed were afire, while his vanity had been wounded to the core. Lady Arabella's icy nature was not so deeply stirred, though she was in a seething passion. More than ever she was set upon bringing Edgar Caswall to her feet. The obstacles she had encountered, the insults she had endured, were only as fuel to the purpose of revenge which consumed her.

As she sought her own rooms in Diana's Grove, she went over the whole subject again and again, always finding in the face of Lilla Watford a key to a problem which puzzled her – the problem of a way to turn Caswall's powers – his very existence – to aid her purpose.

When in her boudoir, she wrote a note, taking so much trouble over it that she destroyed, and rewrote, till her dainty waste-basket was half-full of torn sheets of notepaper. When quite satisfied, she copied out the last sheet afresh, and then carefully burned all the spoiled fragments. She put the copied note in an emblazoned envelope, and directed it to Edgar Caswall at Castra Regis. This she sent off by one of her grooms. The letter ran:

"*Dear Mr. Caswall,*

"I want to have a chat with you on a subject in which I believe you are interested. Will you kindly call for me one day after lunch – say at three or four o'clock, and we can walk a little way together. Only as far as Mercy Farm, where I want to see Lilla and Mimi Watford. We can take a cup of tea at the Farm. Do not bring your African servant with you, as I am afraid his face frightens the girls. After all, he is not pretty, is he? I have an idea you will be pleased with your visit this time.

"Yours sincerely, *Arabella March.*"

At half-past three next day, Edgar Caswall called at Diana's

Grove. Lady Arabella met him on the roadway outside the gate. She wished to take the servants into her confidence as little as possible. She turned when she saw him coming, and walked beside him towards Mercy Farm, keeping step with him as they walked. When they got near Mercy, she turned and looked around her, expecting to see Oolanga or some sign of him. He was, however, not visible. He had received from his master peremptory orders to keep out of sight – an order for which the African scored a new offence up against her. They found Lilla and Mimi at home and seemingly glad to see them, though both the girls were surprised at the visit coming so soon after the other.

The proceedings were a repetition of the battle of souls of the former visit. On this occasion, however, Edgar Caswall had only the presence of Lady Arabella to support him – Oolanga being absent; but Mimi lacked the support of Adam Salton, which had been of such effective service before. This time the struggle for supremacy of will was longer and more determined. Caswall felt that if he could not achieve supremacy he had better give up the idea, so all his pride was enlisted against Mimi. When they had been waiting for the door to be opened, Lady Arabella, believing in a sudden attack, had said to him in a low voice, which somehow carried conviction:

"This time you should win. Mimi is, after all, only a woman. Show her no mercy. That is weakness. Fight her, beat her, trample on her – kill her if need be. She stands in your way, and I hate her. Never take your eyes off her. Never mind Lilla – she is afraid of you. You are already her master. Mimi will try to make you look at her cousin. There lies defeat. Let nothing take your attention from Mimi, and you will win. If she is overcoming you, take my hand and hold it hard whilst you are looking into her eyes. If she is too strong for you, I shall interfere. I'll make a diversion, and under cover of it you must retire unbeaten, even if not victorious. Hush! they are coming."

The two girls came to the door together. Strange sounds were coming up over the Brow from the west. It was the rustling and crackling of the dry reeds and rushes from the low lands. The season had been an unusually dry one. Also the strong east wind was helping forward enormous flocks of birds, most of them pigeons with white cowls. Not only were their wings whirring, but their cooing was plainly audible. From such a multitude of birds the mass of sound, individually small, assumed the volume of a storm. Surprised at the influx of birds, to which they had been strangers so long, they all looked towards Castra Regis, from whose high tower the great kite had been flying as usual. But even as they looked, the cord broke, and the great kite fell headlong in a series of sweeping dives. Its own weight, and the aerial force opposed to it, which caused it to rise, combined with the strong easterly breeze, had been too much for the great length of cord holding it.

Somehow, the mishap to the kite gave new hope to Mimi. It was as though the side issues had been shorn away, so that the main struggle was thenceforth on simpler lines. She had a feeling in her heart, as though some religious chord had been newly touched. It may, of course, have been that with the renewal of the bird voices a fresh courage, a fresh belief in the good issue of the struggle came too. In the misery of silence, from which they had all suffered for so long, any new train of thought was almost bound to be a boon. As the inrush of birds continued, their wings beating against the crackling rushes, Lady Arabella grew pale, and almost fainted.

"What is that?" she asked suddenly.

To Mimi, born and bred in Siam, the sound was strangely like an exaggeration of the sound produced by a snake-charmer.

Edgar Caswall was the first to recover from the interruption of the falling kite. After a few minutes he seemed to have quite recovered his *sang froid*, and was able to use his brains to the end which he had in view. Mimi too quickly recovered herself, but from a different cause. With her it was a deep religious conviction that the struggle round her was of the powers of Good and Evil, and that Good was triumphing. The very appearance of the snowy birds, with the cowls of Saint Columba, heightened the impression. With this conviction strong upon her, she continued the strange battle with fresh vigour. She seemed to tower over Caswall, and he to give back before her oncoming. Once again her vigorous passes drove him to the door. He was just going out backward when Lady Arabella, who had been gazing at him with fixed eyes, caught his hand and tried to stop his movement. She was, however, unable to do any good, and so, holding hands, they passed out together. As they did so, the strange music which had so alarmed Lady Arabella suddenly stopped. Instinctively they all looked towards the tower of Castra Regis, and saw that the workmen had refixed the kite, which had risen again and was beginning to float out to its former station.

As they were looking, the door opened and Michael Watford came into the room. By that time all had recovered their self-possession, and there was nothing out of the common to attract his attention. As he came in, seeing inquiring looks all around him, he said:

"The new influx of birds is only the annual migration of pigeons from Africa. I am told that it will soon be over."

The second victory of Mimi Watford made Edgar Caswall more moody than ever. He felt thrown back on himself, and this, added to his absorbing interest in the hope of a victory of his mesmeric powers, became a deep and settled purpose of revenge. The chief object of his animosity was, of course, Mimi, whose will had overcome his, but it was obscured in greater or lesser degree by all who had opposed him. Lilla was next to Mimi in his hate – Lilla, the harmless, tender-hearted, sweet-natured girl, whose heart was so full of love for all things that in it was no room for the passions of ordinary life – whose nature resembled those doves of St. Columba, whose colour she wore, whose appearance she reflected. Adam Salton came next – after a gap; for against him Caswall had no direct animosity. He regarded him as an interference, a difficulty to be got rid of or destroyed. The young Australian had been so discreet that the most he had against him was his knowledge of what had been. Caswall did not understand him, and to such a nature as his, ignorance was a cause of alarm, of dread.

Caswall resumed his habit of watching the great kite straining at its cord, varying his vigils in this way by a further examination of the mysterious treasures of his house, especially Mesmer's chest. He sat much on the roof of the tower, brooding over his thwarted passion. The vast extent of his possessions, visible to him at that altitude, might, one would have thought, have restored some of his complacency. But the very extent of his ownership, thus perpetually brought before him, created a fresh sense of grievance. How was it, he thought, that with so much at command that others wished for, he could not achieve the dearest wishes of his heart?

In this state of intellectual and moral depravity, he found a solace in the renewal of his experiments with the mechanical powers of the kite. For a couple of weeks he did not see Lady Arabella, who was always on the watch for a chance of meeting him; neither did he see the Watford girls, who studiously kept out of his way. Adam Salton simply marked time, keeping ready to deal with anything that might affect his friends. He called at the farm and heard from Mimi of the last battle of wills, but it had only one consequence. He got from Ross several more mongooses, including a second king-cobra-killer, which he generally carried with him in its box whenever he walked out.

Mr. Caswall's experiments with the kite went on successfully. Each day he tried the lifting of greater weight, and it seemed almost as if the machine had a sentience of its own, which was increasing with the obstacles placed before it. All this time the kite hung in the sky at an enormous height. The wind was steadily from the north, so the trend of the kite was to the south. All day long, runners of increasing magnitude were sent up. These were only of paper or thin cardboard, or leather, or other flexible materials. The great height at which the kite hung made a great concave curve in the string, so that as the runners went up they made a flapping sound. If one laid a finger on the string, the sound answered to the flapping of the runner in a sort of hollow intermittent murmur. Edgar Caswall, who was now wholly obsessed by the kite and all belonging to it, found a distinct resemblance between that intermittent rumble and the snake-charming music produced by the pigeons flying through the dry reeds.

One day he made a discovery in Mesmer's chest which he thought he would utilise with regard to the runners. This was a great length of wire, "fine as human hair," coiled round a finely made wheel, which ran to a wondrous distance freely, and as lightly. He tried this on runners, and found it work admirably. Whether the runner was alone, or carried something much more weighty than itself, it worked equally well. Also it was strong enough and light enough to draw back the runner without undue strain. He tried this a good many times successfully, but it was now growing dusk and he found some difficulty in keeping the runner in sight. So he looked for something heavy enough to keep it still. He placed the Egyptian image of Bes on the fine wire, which crossed the wooden ledge which protected it. Then, the darkness growing, he went indoors and forgot all about it.

He had a strange feeling of uneasiness that night – not sleeplessness, for he seemed conscious of being asleep. At daylight he rose, and as usual looked out for the kite. He did not see it in its usual position in the sky, so looked round the points of the compass. He was more than astonished when presently he saw the missing kite struggling as usual against the controlling cord. But it had gone to the further side of the tower, and now hung and strained *against the wind* to the north. He thought it so strange that he determined to investigate the phenomenon, and to say nothing about it in the meantime.

In his many travels, Edgar Caswall had been accustomed to use the sextant, and was now an expert in the matter. By the aid of this and other instruments, he was able to fix the position of the kite and the point over which it hung. He was startled to find that exactly under it – so far as he could ascertain – was Diana's Grove. He had an inclination to take Lady Arabella into his confidence in the matter, but he thought better of it and wisely refrained. For some reason which he did not try to explain to himself, he was glad of his silence, when, on the following morning, he found, on looking out, that the point over which the kite then hovered was Mercy Farm. When he had verified this with his instruments, he sat before the window of the tower, looking out and thinking. The new locality was more to his liking than the other; but the why of it puzzled him, all the same. He spent the rest of the day in the turret-room, which he did not leave all day. It seemed to him that he was now drawn by forces which he could not control – of which, indeed, he had no knowledge – in directions which he did not understand, and which were without his own volition. In sheer helpless inability to think the problem out satisfactorily, he called up a servant and told him to tell Oolanga that he wanted to see him at once in the turret-room. The answer came back that the African had not been seen since the previous evening.

Caswall was now so irritable that even this small thing upset him. As he was distrait and wanted to talk to somebody, he sent for Simon Chester, who came at once, breathless with hurrying and upset by the unexpected summons. Caswall bade him sit down, and when the old man was in a less uneasy frame of mind, he again asked him if he had ever seen what was in Mesmer's chest or heard it spoken about.

Chester admitted that he had once, in the time of "the then Mr. Edgar," seen the chest open, which, knowing something of its history and guessing more, so upset him that he had fainted. When he recovered, the chest was closed. From that time the then Mr. Edgar had never spoken about it again.

When Caswall asked him to describe what he had seen when the chest was open, he got very agitated, and, despite all his efforts to remain calm, he suddenly went off into a faint. Caswall summoned servants, who applied the usual remedies. Still the old man did not recover. After the lapse of a considerable time, the doctor who had been summoned made his appearance. A glance was sufficient for him to make up his mind. Still, he knelt down by the old man, and made a careful examination. Then he rose to his feet, and in a hushed voice said:

"I grieve to say, sir, that he has passed away."

CHAPTER XV

ON THE TRACK

THOSE WHO HAD SEEN EDGAR Caswall familiarly since his arrival, and had already estimated his cold-blooded nature at something of its true value, were surprised that he took so to heart the death of old Chester. The fact was that not one of them had guessed correctly at his character. They thought, naturally enough, that the concern which he felt was that of a master for a faithful old servant of his family. They little thought that it was merely the selfish expression of his disappointment, that he had thus lost the only remaining clue to an interesting piece of family history – one which was now and would be for ever wrapped in mystery. Caswall knew enough about the life of his ancestor in Paris to wish to know more fully and more thoroughly all that had been. The period covered by that ancestor's life in Paris was one inviting every form of curiosity.

Lady Arabella, who had her own game to play, saw in the *metier* of sympathetic friend, a series of meetings with the man she wanted to secure. She made the first use of the opportunity the day after old Chester's death; indeed, as soon as the news had filtered in through the back door of Diana's Grove. At that meeting, she played her part so well that even Caswall's cold nature was impressed.

Oolanga was the only one who did not credit her with at least some sense of fine feeling in the matter. In emotional, as in other matters, Oolanga was distinctly a utilitarian, and as he could not understand anyone feeling grief except for his own suffering, pain, or for the loss of money, he could not understand anyone simulating such an emotion except for show intended to deceive. He thought that she had come to Castra Regis again for the opportunity of stealing something, and was determined that on this occasion the chance of pressing his advantage over her should not pass. He felt, therefore, that the occasion was one for extra carefulness in the watching of all that went on. Ever since he had come to the conclusion that Lady Arabella was trying to steal the treasure-chest, he suspected nearly everyone of the same design, and made it a point to watch all suspicious persons and places. As Adam was engaged on his own researches regarding Lady Arabella, it was only natural that there should be some crossing of each other's tracks. This is what did actually happen.

Adam had gone for an early morning survey of the place in which he was interested, taking with him the mongoose in its box. He arrived at the gate of Diana's Grove just as Lady Arabella was preparing to set out for Castra Regis on what she considered her mission of comfort. Seeing Adam from her window going through the shadows of the trees round the gate, she thought that he must be engaged on some purpose similar to her own. So, quickly making her toilet, she quietly left the house, and, taking advantage of every shadow and substance which could hide her, followed him on his walk.

Oolanga, the experienced tracker, followed her, but succeeded in hiding his movements better than she did. He saw that Adam had on his shoulder a mysterious box, which he took to contain something valuable. Seeing that Lady Arabella was secretly following Adam, he was confirmed in this idea. His mind – such as it was – was fixed on her trying to steal, and he credited her at once with making use of this new opportunity.

In his walk, Adam went into the grounds of Castra Regis, and Oolanga saw her follow him with great secrecy. He feared to go closer, as now on both sides of him were enemies who might make discovery. When he realised that Lady Arabella was bound for the Castle, he devoted himself to following her with single-ness of purpose. He therefore missed seeing that Adam branched off the track and returned to the high road.

That night Edgar Caswall had slept badly. The tragic occurrence of the day was on his mind, and he kept waking and thinking of it. After an early breakfast, he sat at the open window watching the kite and thinking of many things. From his room he could see all round the neighbourhood, but the two places that interested him most were Mercy Farm and Diana's Grove. At first the move-ments about those spots were of a humble kind – those that be-long to domestic service or agricultural needs – the opening of doors and windows, the sweeping and brushing, and generally the restoration of habitual order.

From his high window – whose height made it a screen from the observation of others – he saw the chain of watchers move into his own grounds, and then presently break up – Adam Salton going one way, and Lady Arabella, followed by the African*, an-other. Then Oolanga disappeared amongst the trees; but Caswall could see that he was still watching. Lady Arabella, after looking around her, slipped in by the open door, and he could, of course, see her no longer.

Presently, however, he heard a light tap at his door, then the door opened slowly, and he could see the flash of Lady Arabella's white dress through the opening.

CHAPTER XVI

A VISIT OF SYMPATHY

CASWALL WAS GENUINELY SURPRISED when he saw Lady Ara-bella, though he need not have been, after what had already oc-curred in the same way. The look of surprise on his face was so much greater than Lady Arabella had expected – though she thought she was prepared to meet anything that might occur – that she stood still, in sheer amazement. Cold-blooded as she was and ready for all social emergencies, she was nonplussed how to go on. She was plucky, however, and began to speak at once, al-though she had not the slightest idea what she was going to say.

"I came to offer you my very warm sympathy with the grief you have so lately experienced."

"My grief? I'm afraid I must be very dull; but I really do not understand."

Already she felt at a disadvantage, and hesitated.

"I mean about the old man who died so suddenly – your old. . . retainer."

Caswall's face relaxed something of its puzzled concentration. "Oh, he was only a servant; and he had over-stayed his three-score and ten years by something like twenty years. He must have been ninety!"

"Still, as an old servant. . ."

Caswall's words were not so cold as their inflection. "I never interfere with servants. He was kept on here merely because he had been so long on the premises. I suppose the steward thought it might make him unpopular if the old fellow had been dismissed."

How on earth was she to proceed on such a task as hers if this was the utmost geniality she could expect? So she at once tried another tack – this time a personal one.

"I am sorry I disturbed you. I am really not unconventional – though certainly no slave to convention. Still there are limits. . . it is bad enough to intrude in this way, and I do not know what you can say or think of the time selected, for the intrusion."

After all, Edgar Caswall was a gentleman by custom and habit, so he rose to the occasion.

"I can only say, Lady Arabella, that you are always welcome at any time you may deign to honour my house with your presence."

She smiled at him sweetly.

"Thank you *so* much. You *do* put one at ease. My breach of convention makes me glad rather than sorry. I feel that I can open my heart to you about anything."

Forthwith she proceeded to tell him about Oolanga and his strange suspicions of her honesty. Caswall laughed and made her explain all the details. His final comment was enlightening.

"Let me give you a word of advice: If you have the slightest fault to find with that infernal nigger, shoot him at sight. A swelled-headed nigger, with a bee in his bonnet, is one of the worst difficulties in the world to deal with. So better make a clean job of it, and wipe him out at once!"

"But what about the law, Mr. Caswall?"

"Oh, the law doesn't concern itself much about dead niggers. A few more or less do not matter. To my mind it's rather a relief!"

"I'm afraid of you," was her only comment, made with a sweet smile and in a soft voice.

"All right," he said, "let us leave it at that. Anyhow, we shall be rid of one of them!"

"I don't love niggers any more than you do," she replied, "and I suppose one mustn't be too particular where that sort of cleaning up is concerned." Then she changed in voice and manner, and asked genially: "And now tell me, am I forgiven?"

"You are, dear lady – if there is anything to forgive."

As he spoke, seeing that she had moved to go, he came to the door with her, and in the most natural way accompanied her downstairs. He passed through the hall with her and down the avenue. As he went back to the house, she smiled to herself.

"Well, that is all right. I don't think the morning has been altogether thrown away."

And she walked slowly back to Diana's Grove.

Adam Salton followed the line of the Brow, and refreshed his memory as to the various localities. He got home to Lesser Hill just as Sir Nathaniel was beginning lunch. Mr. Salton had gone to Walsall to keep an early appointment; so he was all alone. When the meal was over – seeing in Adam's face that he had something to speak about – he followed into the study and shut the door.

When the two men had lighted their pipes, Sir Nathaniel began.

"I have remembered an interesting fact about Diana's Grove – there is, I have long understood, some strange mystery about that house. It may be of some interest, or it may be trivial, in such a tangled skein as we are trying to unravel."

"Please tell me all you know or suspect. To begin, then, of what sort is the mystery – physical, mental, moral, historical, scientific, occult? Any kind of hint will help me."

"Quite right. I shall try to tell you what I think; but I have not put my thoughts on the subject in sequence, so you must forgive me if due order is not observed in my narration. I suppose you have seen the house at Diana's Grove?"

"The outside of it; but I have that in my mind's eye, and I can fit into my memory whatever you may mention."

"The house is very old – probably the first house of some sort that stood there was in the time of the Romans. This was probably renewed – perhaps several times at later periods. The house stands, or, rather, used to stand here when Mercia was a kingdom – I do not suppose that the basement can be later than the Norman Conquest. Some years ago, when I was President of the Mercian Archaeological Society, I went all over it very carefully. This was when it was purchased by Captain March. The house had then been done up, so as to be suitable for the bride. The basement is very strong, – almost as strong and as heavy as if it had been intended as a fortress. There are a whole series of rooms deep underground. One of them in particular struck me. The room itself is of considerable size, but the masonry is more than massive. In the middle of the room is a sunk well, built up to floor level and evidently going deep underground. There is no windlass nor any trace of there ever having been any – no rope – nothing. Now, we know that the Romans had wells of immense depth, from which the water was lifted by the 'old rag rope'; that at Woodhull used to be nearly a thousand feet. Here, then, we have simply an enormously deep well-hole. The door of the room was massive, and was fastened with a lock nearly a foot square. It was evidently intended for some kind of protection to someone or something; but no one in those days had ever heard of anyone having been allowed even to see the room. All this is *e propos* of a suggestion on my part that the well-hole was a way by which the White Worm (whatever it was) went and came. At that time I would have had a search made – even excavation if necessary – at my own expense, but all suggestions were met with a prompt and explicit negative. So, of course, I took no further step in the matter. Then it died out of recollection – even of mine."

"Do you remember, sir," asked Adam, "what was the appearance of the room where the well-hole was? Was there furniture – in fact, any sort of thing in the room?"

"The only thing I remember was a sort of green light – very clouded, very dim – which came up from the well. Not a fixed light, but intermittent and irregular – quite unlike anything I had ever seen."

"Do you remember how you got into the well-room? Was there a separate door from outside, or was there any interior room or passage which opened into it?"

"I think there must have been some room with a way into it. I remember going up some steep steps; they must have been worn smooth by long use or something of the kind, for I could hardly keep my feet as I went up. Once I stumbled and nearly fell into the well-hole."

"Was there anything strange about the place – any queer smell, for instance?"

"Queer smell – yes! Like bilge or a rank swamp. It was distinctly nauseating; when I came out I felt as if I had just been going to be sick. I shall try back on my visit and see if I can recall any more of what I saw or felt."

"Then perhaps, sir, later in the day you will tell me anything you may chance to recollect."

"I shall be delighted, Adam. If your uncle has not returned by then, I'll join you in the study after dinner, and we can resume this interesting chat."

CHAPTER XVII

THE MYSTERY OF "THE GROVE"

THAT AFTERNOON ADAM DECIDED to do a little exploring. As he passed through the wood outside the gate of Diana's Grove, he thought he saw the African's face for an instant. So he went deeper into the undergrowth, and followed along parallel to the avenue to the house. He was glad that there was no workman or servant about, for he did not care that any of Lady Arabella's people should find him wandering about her grounds. Taking advantage of the denseness of the trees, he came close to the house and skirted round it. He was repaid for his trouble, for on the far side of the house, close to where the rocky frontage of the cliff fell away, he saw Oolanga crouched behind the irregular trunk of a great oak. The man was so intent on watching someone, or something, that he did not guard against being himself watched. This suited Adam, for he could thus make scrutiny at will.

The thick wood, though the trees were mostly of small girth, threw a heavy shadow, so that the steep declension, in front of which grew the tree behind which the African lurked, was almost in darkness. Adam drew as close as he could, and was amazed to see a patch of light on the ground before him; when he realised what it was, he was determined, more than ever to follow on his quest. The African* had a dark lantern in his hand, and was throwing the light down the steep incline. The glare showed a series of stone steps, which ended in a low-lying heavy iron door fixed against the side of the house. All the strange things he had heard from Sir Nathaniel, and all those, little and big, which he had himself noticed, crowded into his mind in a chaotic way. Instinctively he took refuge behind a thick oak stem, and set himself down, to watch what might occur.

After a short time it became apparent that the African was trying to find out what was behind the heavy door. There was no way of looking in, for the door fitted tight into the massive stone slabs. The only opportunity for the entrance of light was through a small hole between the great stones above the door. This hole was too high up to look through from the ground level. Oolanga, having tried standing tiptoe on the highest point near, and holding the lantern as high as he could, threw the light round the edges of the door to see if he could find anywhere a hole or a flaw in the metal through which he could obtain a glimpse. Foiled in this, he brought from the shrubbery a plank, which he leant against the top of the door and then climbed up with great dexterity. This did not bring him near enough to the window-hole to look in, or even to throw the light of the lantern through it, so he climbed down and carried the plank back to the place from which he had got it. Then he concealed himself near the iron door and waited, manifestly with the intent of remaining there till someone came near. Presently Lady Arabella, moving noiselessly through the shade, approached the door. When he saw her close enough to touch it, Oolanga stepped forward from his concealment, and spoke in a whisper, which through the gloom sounded like a hiss.

"I want to see you, missy – soon and secret."

"What do you want?"

"You know well, missy; I told you already."

She turned on him with blazing eyes, the green tint in them glowing like emeralds.

"Come, none of that. If there is anything sensible which you wish to say to me, you can see me here, just where we are, at seven o'clock."

He made no reply in words, but, putting the backs of his hands together, bent lower and lower till his forehead touched the earth. Then he rose and went slowly away.

Adam Salton, from his hiding-place, saw and wondered. In a few minutes he moved from his place and went home to Lesser Hill, fully determined that seven o'clock would find him in some hidden place behind Diana's Grove.

At a little before seven Adam stole softly out of the house and took the back-way to the rear of Diana's Grove. The place seemed silent and deserted, so he took the opportunity of concealing himself near the spot whence he had seen Oolanga trying to investigate whatever was concealed behind the iron door. He waited, perfectly still, and at last saw a gleam of white passing soundlessly through the undergrowth. He was not surprised when he recognised the colour of Lady Arabella's dress. She came close and waited, with her face to the iron door. From some place of concealment near at hand Oolanga appeared, and came close to her. Adam noticed, with surprised amusement, that over his shoulder was the box with the mongoose. Of course the African did not know that he was seen by anyone, least of all by the man whose property he had with him.

Silent-footed as he was, Lady Arabella heard him coming, and turned to meet him. It was somewhat hard to see in the gloom, for, as usual, he was all in black, only his collar and cuffs showing white. Lady Arabella opened the conversation which ensued between the two.

"What do you want? To rob me, or murder me?"

"No, to lub you!"

This frightened her a little, and she tried to change the tone.

"Is that a coffin you have with you? If so, you are wasting your time. It would not hold me."

When a native* suspects he is being laughed at, all the ferocity of his nature comes to the front; and this man was of the lowest kind.

"Dis ain't no coffin for nobody. Dis box is for you. Somefin you lub. Me give him to you!"

Still anxious to keep off the subject of affection, on which she believed him to have become crazed, she made another effort to keep his mind elsewhere.

"Is this why you want to see me?" He nodded. "Then come round to the other door. But be quiet. I have no desire to be seen so close to my own house in conversation with a – a – a nigger like you!"

She had chosen the word deliberately. She wished to meet his passion with another kind. Such would, at all events, help to keep him quiet. In the deep gloom she could not see the anger which suffused his face. Rolling eyeballs and grinding teeth are, however, sufficient signs of anger to be decipherable in the dark. She moved round the corner of the house to her right. Oolanga was following her, when she stopped him by raising her hand.

"No, not that door," she said; "that is not for niggers. The other door will do well enough for you!"

Lady Arabella took in her hand a small key which hung at the end of her watch-chain, and moved to a small door, low down, round the corner, and a little downhill from the edge of the Brow. Oolanga, in obedience to her gesture, went back to the iron door. Adam looked carefully at the mongoose box as the African went by, and was glad to see that it was intact. Unconsciously, as he looked, he fingered the key that was in his waistcoat pocket. When Oolanga was out of sight, Adam hurried after Lady Arabella.

CHAPTER XVIII
EXIT OOLANGA

THE WOMAN TURNED SHARPLY as Adam touched her shoulder.

"One moment whilst we are alone. You had better not trust that man!"* he whispered.

Her answer was crisp and concise:

"I don't."

"Forewarned is forearmed. Tell me if you will – it is for your own protection. Why do you mistrust him?"

"My friend, you have no idea of that man's impudence. Would you believe that he wants me to marry him?"

"No!" said Adam incredulously, amused in spite of himself.

"Yes, and wanted to bribe me to do it by sharing a chest of treasure – at least, he thought it was – stolen from Mr. Caswall. Why do you distrust him, Mr. Salton?"

"Did you notice that box he had slung on his shoulder? That belongs to me. I left it in the gun-room when I went to lunch. He must have crept in and stolen it. Doubtless he thinks that it, too, is full of treasure."

"He does!"

"How on earth do you know?" asked Adam.

"A little while ago he offered to give it to me – another bribe to accept him. Faugh! I am ashamed to tell you such a thing. The beast!"

Whilst they had been speaking, she had opened the door, a narrow iron one, well hung, for it opened easily and closed tightly without any creaking or sound of any kind. Within all was dark; but she entered as freely and with as little misgiving or restraint as if it had been broad daylight. For Adam, there was just sufficient green light from somewhere for him to see that there was a broad flight of heavy stone steps leading upward; but Lady Arabella, after shutting the door behind her, when it closed tightly without a clang, tripped up the steps lightly and swiftly. For an instant all was dark, but there came again the faint green light which enabled him to see the outlines of things. Another iron door, narrow like the first and fairly high, led into another large room, the walls of which were of massive stones, so closely joined together as to exhibit only one smooth surface. This presented the appearance of having at one time been polished. On the far side, also smooth like the walls, was the reverse of a wide, but not high, iron door. Here there was a little more light, for the high-up aperture over the door opened to the air.

Lady Arabella took from her girdle another small key, which she inserted in a keyhole in the centre of a massive lock. The great bolt seemed wonderfully hung, for the moment the small key was turned, the bolts of the great lock moved noiselessly and the iron doors swung open. On the stone steps outside stood Oolanga, with the mongoose box slung over his shoulder. Lady Arabella stood a little on one side, and the African, accepting the movement as an invitation, entered in an obsequious way. The moment, however, that he was inside, he gave a quick look around him.

"Much death here – big death. Many deaths. Good, good!"

He sniffed round as if he was enjoying the scent. The matter and manner of his speech were so revolting that instinctively Adam's hand wandered to his revolver, and, with his finger on the trigger, he rested satisfied that he was ready for any emergency.

There was certainly opportunity for the African's* enjoyment, for the open well-hole was almost under his nose, sending up such a stench as almost made Adam sick, though Lady Arabella seemed not to mind it at all. It was like nothing that Adam had ever met with. He compared it with all the noxious experiences he had ever had – the drainage of war hospitals, of slaughter-houses, the refuse of dissecting rooms. None of these was like it, though it had something of them all, with, added, the sourness of chemical waste and the poisonous effluvium of the bilge of a waterlogged ship whereon a multitude of rats had been drowned.

Then, quite unexpectedly, the negro noticed the presence of a third person – Adam Salton! He pulled out a pistol and shot at him, happily missing. Adam was himself usually a quick shot, but this time his mind had been on something else and he was not ready. However, he was quick to carry out an intention, and he was not a coward. In another moment both men were in grips. Beside them was the dark well-hole, with that horrid effluvium stealing up from its mysterious depths.

Adam and Oolanga both had pistols; Lady Arabella, who had not one, was probably the most ready of them all in the theory of shooting, but that being impossible, she made her effort in another way. Gliding forward, she tried to seize the African; but he eluded her grasp, just missing, in doing so, falling into the mysterious hole. As he swayed back to firm foothold, he turned his own gun on her and shot. Instinctively Adam leaped at his assailant; clutching at each other, they tottered on the very brink.

Lady Arabella's anger, now fully awake, was all for Oolanga. She moved towards him with her hands extended, and had just seized him when the catch of the locked box – due to some movement from within – flew open, and the king-cobra-killer flew at her with a venomous fury impossible to describe. As it seized her throat, she caught hold of it, and, with a fury superior to its own, tore it in two just as if it had been a sheet of paper. The strength used for such an act must have been terrific. In an instant, it seemed to spout blood and entrails, and was hurled into the well-hole. In another instant she had seized Oolanga, and with a swift rush had drawn him, her white arms encircling him, down with her into the gaping aperture.

Adam saw a medley of green and red lights blaze in a whirling circle, and as it sank down into the well, a pair of blazing green eyes became fixed, sank lower and lower with frightful rapidity, and disappeared, throwing upward the green light which grew more and more vivid every moment. As the light sank into the noisome depths, there came a shriek which chilled Adam's blood – a prolonged agony of pain and terror which seemed to have no end.

Adam Salton felt that he would never be able to free his mind from the memory of those dreadful moments. The gloom which surrounded that horrible charnel pit, which seemed to go down to the very bowels of the earth, conveyed from far down the sights and sounds of the nethermost hell. The ghastly fate of the African as he sank down to his terrible doom, his black face growing grey with terror, his white eyeballs, now like veined bloodstone, rolling in the helpless extremity of fear. The mysterious green light was in itself a milieu of horror. And through it all the awful cry came up from that fathomless pit, whose entrance was flooded with spots of fresh blood. Even the death of the fearless little snake-killer – so fierce, so frightful, as if stained with a ferocity which told of no living force above earth, but only of the devils of the pit – was only an incident. Adam was in a state of intellectual tumult, which had no parallel in his experience. He tried to rush away from the horrible place; even the baleful green light, thrown up through the gloomy well-shaft, was dying away as its source sank deeper into the primeval ooze. The darkness was closing in on him in overwhelming density – darkness in such a place and with such a memory of it!

He made a wild rush forward – slipt on the steps in some sticky, acrid-smelling mass that felt and smelt like blood, and, falling forward, felt his way into the inner room, where the well-shaft was not. Then he rubbed his eyes in sheer amazement. Up the stone steps from the narrow door by which he had entered, glided the white-clad figure of Lady Arabella, the only colour to be seen on her being blood-marks on her face and hands and throat. Otherwise, she was calm and unruffled, as when earlier she stood aside for him to pass in through the narrow iron door.

CHAPTER XIX

AN ENEMY IN THE DARK

ADAM SALTON WENT FOR A walk before returning to Lesser Hill; he felt that it might be well, not only to steady his nerves, shaken by the horrible scene, but to get his thoughts into some sort of order, so as to be ready to enter on the matter with Sir Nathaniel. He was a little embarrassed as to telling his uncle, for affairs had so vastly progressed beyond his original view that he felt a little doubtful as to what would be the old gentleman's attitude when he should hear of the strange events for the first time. Mr. Salton would certainly not be satisfied at being treated as an outsider with regard to such things, most of which had points of contact with the inmates of his own house. It was with an immense sense of relief that Adam heard that his uncle had telegraphed to the housekeeper that he was detained by business at Walsall, where he would remain for the night; and that he would be back in the morning in time for lunch.

When Adam got home after his walk, he found Sir Nathaniel just going to bed. He did not say anything to him then of what had happened, but contented himself with arranging that they would walk together in the early morning, as he had much to say that would require serious attention.

Strangely enough he slept well, and awoke at dawn with his mind clear and his nerves in their usual unshaken condition. The maid brought up, with his early morning cup of tea, a note which had been found in the letter-box. It was from Lady Arabella, and was evidently intended to put him on his guard as to what he should say about the previous evening.

He read it over carefully several times, before he was satisfied that he had taken in its full import.

"*Dear Mr. Salton,*

"I cannot go to bed until I have written to you, so you must forgive me if I disturb you, and at an unseemly time. Indeed, you must also forgive me if, in trying to do what is right, I err in saying too much or too little. The fact is that I am quite upset and unnerved by all that has happened in this terrible night. I find it difficult even to write; my hands shake so that they are not under control, and I am trembling all over with memory of the horrors we saw enacted before our eyes. I am grieved beyond measure that I should be, however remotely, a cause of this horror coming on you. Forgive me if you can, and do not think too hardly of me. This I ask with confidence, for since we shared together the danger – the very pangs – of death, I feel that we should be to one another something more than mere friends, that I may lean on you and trust you, assured that your sympathy and pity are for me. You really must let me thank you for the friendliness, the help, the confidence, the real aid at a time of deadly danger and deadly fear which you showed me. That awful man – I shall see him for ever in my dreams. His black, malignant face will shut out all memory of sunshine and happiness. I shall eternally see his evil eyes as he threw himself into that well-hole in a vain effort to escape from the consequences of his own misdoing. The more I think of it, the more apparent it seems to me that he had premeditated the whole thing – of course, except his own horrible death.

"Perhaps you have noticed a fur collar I occasionally wear. It is one of my most valued treasures – an ermine collar studded with emeralds. I had often seen the nigger's eyes gleam covetously when he looked at it. Unhappily, I wore it yesterday. That may have been the cause that lured the poor man to his doom. On the very brink of the abyss he tore the collar from my neck – that was the last I saw of him. When he sank into the hole, I was rushing to the iron door, which I pulled behind me. When I heard that soul-sickening yell, which marked his disappearance in the chasm, I was more glad than I can say that my eyes were spared the pain and horror which my ears had to endure.

"When I tore myself out of the negro's grasp as he sank into the well-hole; I realised what freedom meant. Freedom! Freedom! Not only from that noisome prison-house, which has now such a memory, but from the more noisome embrace of that hideous monster. Whilst I live, I shall always thank you for my freedom. A woman must sometimes express her gratitude; otherwise it becomes too great to bear. I am not a sentimental girl, who merely likes to thank a man; I am a woman who knows all, of bad as well as good, that life can give. I have known what it is to love and to lose. But you must not let me bring any unhappiness into your life. I must live on – as I have lived – alone, and, in addition, bear with other woes the memory of this latest insult and horror. In the meantime, I must get away as quickly as possible from Diana's Grove. In the morning I shall go up to town, where I shall remain for a week – I cannot stay longer, as business affairs demand my presence here. I think, however, that a week in the rush of busy London, surrounded with multitudes of commonplace people, will help to soften – I cannot expect total obliteration – the terrible images of the bygone night. When I can sleep easily – which will be, I hope, after a day or two – I shall be fit to return home and take up again the burden which will, I suppose, always be with me.

"I shall be most happy to see you on my return – or earlier, if my good fortune sends you on any errand to London. I shall stay at the Mayfair Hotel. In that busy spot we may forget some of the dangers and horrors we have shared together. Adieu, and thank you, again and again, for all your kindness and consideration to me.

"*Arabella Marsh.*"

Adam was surprised by this effusive epistle, but he determined to say nothing of it to Sir Nathaniel until he should have thought it well over. When Adam met Sir Nathaniel at breakfast, he was glad that he had taken time to turn things over in his mind. The result had been that not only was he familiar with the facts in all their bearings, but he had already so far differentiated them that he was able to arrange them in his own mind according to their values. Breakfast had been a silent function, so it did not interfere in any way with the process of thought.

So soon as the door was closed, Sir Nathaniel began:

"I see, Adam, that something has occurred, and that you have much to tell me."

"That is so, sir. I suppose I had better begin by telling you all I know – all that has happened since I left you yesterday?"

Accordingly Adam gave him details of all that had happened during the previous evening. He confined himself rigidly to the narration of circumstances, taking care not to colour events by any comment of his own, or any opinion of the meaning of things which he did not fully understand. At first, Sir Nathaniel seemed disposed to ask questions, but shortly gave this up when he recognised that the narration was concise and self-explanatory. Thenceforth, he contented himself with quick looks and glances, easily interpreted, or by some acquiescent motions of his hands, when such could be convenient, to emphasise his idea of the correctness of any inference. Until Adam ceased speaking, having evidently come to an end of what he had to say with regard to this section of his story, the elder man made no comment whatever. Even when Adam took from his pocket Lady Arabella's letter, with the manifest intention of reading it, he did not make any comment. Finally, when Adam folded up the letter and put it, in its envelope, back in his pocket, as an intimation that he had now quite finished, the old diplomatist carefully made a few notes in his pocket-book.

"Your narrative, my dear Adam, is altogether admirable. I think I may now take it that we are both well versed in the actual facts, and that our conference had better take the shape of a mutual exchange of ideas. Let us both ask questions as they may arise; and I do not doubt that we shall arrive at some enlightening conclusions."

"Will you kindly begin, sir? I do not doubt that, with your longer experience, you will be able to dissipate some of the fog which envelops certain of the things which we have to consider."

"I hope so, my dear boy. For a beginning, then, let me say that Lady Arabella's letter makes clear some things which she intended – and also some things which she did not intend. But, before I begin to draw deductions, let me ask you a few questions. Adam, are you heart-whole, quite heart-whole, in the matter of Lady Arabella?"

His companion answered at once, each looking the other straight in the eyes during question and answer.

"Lady Arabella, sir, is a charming woman, and I should have deemed it a privilege to meet her – to talk to her – even – since I am in the confessional – to flirt a little with her. But if you mean to ask if my affections are in any way engaged, I can emphatically answer 'No!' – as indeed you will understand when presently I give you the reason. Apart from that, there are the unpleasant details we discussed the other day."

"Could you – would you mind giving me the reason now? It will help us to understand what is before us, in the way of difficulty."

"Certainly, sir. My reason, on which I can fully depend, is that I love another woman!"

"That clinches it. May I offer my good wishes, and, I hope, my congratulations?"

"I am proud of your good wishes, sir, and I thank you for them. But it is too soon for congratulations – the lady does not even know my hopes yet. Indeed, I hardly knew them myself, as definite, till this moment."

"I take it then, Adam, that at the right time I may be allowed to know who the lady is?"

Adam laughed a low, sweet laugh, such as ripples from a happy heart.

"There need not be an hour's, a minute's delay. I shall be glad to share my secret with you, sir. The lady, sir, whom I am so happy as to love, and in whom my dreams of life-long happiness are centred, is Mimi Watford!"

"Then, my dear Adam, I need not wait to offer congratulations. She is indeed a very charming young lady. I do not think I ever saw a girl who united in such perfection the qualities of strength of character and sweetness of disposition. With all my heart, I congratulate you. Then I may take it that my question as to your heart-wholeness is answered in the affirmative?"

"Yes; and now, sir, may I ask in turn why the question?"

"Certainly! I asked because it seems to me that we are coming to a point where my questions might be painful to you."

"It is not merely that I love Mimi, but I have reason to look on Lady Arabella as her enemy," Adam continued.

"Her enemy?"

"Yes. A rank and unscrupulous enemy who is bent on her destruction."

Sir Nathaniel went to the door, looked outside it and returned, locking it carefully behind him.

CHAPTER XX

METABOLISM

"AM I LOOKING GRAVE?" asked Sir Nathaniel inconsequently when he re-entered the room.

"You certainly are, sir."

"We little thought when first we met that we should be drawn into such a vortex. Already we are mixed up in robbery, and probably murder, but – a thousand times worse than all the crimes in the calendar – in an affair of ghastly mystery which has no bottom and no end – with forces of the most unnerving kind, which had their origin in an age when the world was different from the world which we know. We are going back to the origin of superstition – to an age when dragons tore each other in their slime. We must fear nothing – no conclusion, however improbable, almost impossible it may be. Life and death is hanging on our judgment, not only for ourselves, but for others whom we love. Remember, I count on you as I hope you count on me."

"I do, with all confidence."

"Then," said Sir Nathaniel, "let us think justly and boldly and fear nothing, however terrifying it may seem. I suppose I am to take as exact in every detail your account of all the strange things which happened whilst you were in Diana's Grove?"

"So far as I know, yes. Of course I may be mistaken in recollection of some detail or another, but I am certain that in the main what I have said is correct."

"You feel sure that you saw Lady Arabella seize the negro round the neck, and drag him down with her into the hole?"

"Absolutely certain, sir, otherwise I should have gone to her assistance."

"We have, then, an account of what happened from an eye-witness whom we trust – that is yourself. We have also another account, written by Lady Arabella under her own hand. These two accounts do not agree. Therefore we must take it that one of the two is lying."

"Apparently, sir."

"And that Lady Arabella is the liar!"

"Apparently – as I am not."

"We must, therefore, try to find a reason for her lying. She has nothing to fear from Oolanga, who is dead. Therefore the only reason which could actuate her would be to convince someone else that she was blameless. This 'someone' could not be you, for you had the evidence of your own eyes. There was no one else present; therefore it must have been an absent person."

"That seems beyond dispute, sir."

"There is only one other person whose good opinion she could wish to keep – Edgar Caswall. He is the only one who fills the bill. Her lies point to other things besides the death of the African. She evidently wanted it to be accepted that his falling into the well was his own act. I cannot suppose that she expected to convince you, the eye-witness; but if she wished later on to spread the story, it was wise of her to try to get your acceptance of it."

"That is so!"

"Then there were other matters of untruth. That, for instance, of the ermine collar embroidered with emeralds. If an understandable reason be required for this, it would be to draw attention away from the green lights which were seen in the room, and especially in the well-hole. Any unprejudiced person would accept the green lights to be the eyes of a great snake, such as tradition pointed to living in the well-hole. In fine, therefore, Lady Arabella wanted the general belief to be that there was no snake of the kind in Diana's Grove. For my own part, I don't believe in a partial liar – this art does not deal in veneer; a liar is a liar right through. Self-interest may prompt falsity of the tongue; but if one prove to be a liar, nothing that he says can ever be believed. This leads us to the conclusion that because she said or inferred that there was no snake, we should look for one – and expect to find it, too.

"Now let me digress. I live, and have for many years lived, in Derbyshire, a county more celebrated for its caves than any other county in England. I have been through them all, and am familiar with every turn of them; as also with other great caves in Kentucky, in France, in Germany, and a host of other places – in many of these are tremendously deep caves of narrow aperture, which are valued by intrepid explorers, who descend narrow gullets of abysmal depth – and sometimes never return. In many of the caverns in the Peak I am convinced that some of the smaller passages were used in primeval times as the lairs of some of the great serpents of legend and tradition. It may have been that such caverns were formed in the usual geologic way – bubbles or flaws in the earth's crust – which were later used by the monsters of the period of the young world. It may have been, of course, that some of them were worn originally by water; but in time they all found a use when suitable for living monsters.

"This brings us to another point, more difficult to accept and understand than any other requiring belief in a base not usually accepted, or indeed entered on – whether such abnormal growths could have ever changed in their nature. Some day the study of metabolism may progress so far as to enable us to accept structural changes proceeding from an intellectual or moral base. We may lean towards a belief that great animal strength may be a sound base for changes of all sorts. If this be so, what could be a more fitting subject than primeval monsters whose strength was such as to allow a survival of thousands of years? We do not know yet if brain can increase and develop independently of other parts of the living structure.

"After all, the mediaeval belief in the Philosopher's Stone which could transmute metals, has its counterpart in the accepted theory of metabolism which changes living tissue. In an age of investigation like our own, when we are returning to science as the base of wonders – almost of miracles – we should be slow to refuse to accept facts, however impossible they may seem to be.

"Let us suppose a monster of the early days of the world – a dragon of the prime – of vast age running into thousands of years, to whom had been conveyed in some way – it matters not – a brain just sufficient for the beginning of growth. Suppose the monster to be of incalculable size and of a strength quite abnormal – a veritable incarnation of animal strength. Suppose this animal is allowed to remain in one place, thus being removed from accidents of interrupted development; might not, would not this creature, in process of time – ages, if necessary – have that rudimentary intelligence developed? There is no impossibility in this; it is only the natural process of evolution. In the beginning, the instincts of animals are confined to alimentation, self-protection, and the multiplication of their species. As time goes on and the needs of life become more complex, power follows need. We have been long accustomed to consider growth as applied almost exclusively to size in its various aspects. But Nature, who has no doctrinaire ideas, may equally apply it to concentration. A developing thing may expand in any given way or form. Now, it is a scientific law that increase implies gain and loss of various kinds; what a thing gains in one direction it may lose in another. May it not be that Mother Nature may deliberately encourage decrease as well as increase – that it may be an axiom that what is gained in concentration is lost in size? Take, for instance, monsters that tradition has accepted and localised, such as the Worm of Lambton or that of Spindleston Heugh. If such a creature were, by its own process of metabolism, to change much of its bulk for intellectual growth, we should at once arrive at a new class of creature – more dangerous, perhaps, than the world has ever had any experience of – a force which can think, which has no soul and no morals, and therefore no acceptance of responsibility. A snake would be a good illustration of this, for it is cold-blooded, and therefore removed from the temptations which often weaken or restrict warm-blooded creatures. If, for instance, the Worm of Lambton – if such ever existed – were guided to its own ends by an organised intelligence capable of expansion, what form of creature could we imagine which would equal it in potentialities of evil? Why, such a being would devastate a whole country. Now, all these things require much thought, and we want to apply the knowledge usefully, and we should therefore be exact. Would it not be well to resume the subject later in the day?"

"I quite agree, sir. I am in a whirl already; and want to attend carefully to what you say; so that I may try to digest it."

Both men seemed fresher and better for the "easy," and when they met in the afternoon each of them had something to contribute to the general stock of information. Adam, who was by nature of a more militant disposition than his elderly friend, was glad to see that the conference at once assumed a practical trend. Sir Nathaniel recognised this, and, like an old diplomatist, turned it to present use.

"Tell me now, Adam, what is the outcome, in your own mind, of our conversation?"

"That the whole difficulty already assumes practical shape; but with added dangers, that at first I did not imagine."

"What is the practical shape, and what are the added dangers? I am not disputing, but only trying to clear my own ideas by the consideration of yours – "

So Adam went on:

"In the past, in the early days of the world, there were monsters who were so vast that they could exist for thousands of years. Some of them must have overlapped the Christian era. They may have progressed intellectually in process of time. If they had in any way so progressed, or even got the most rudimentary form of brain, they would be the most dangerous things that ever were in the world. Tradition says that one of these monsters lived in the Marsh of the East, and came up to a cave in Diana's Grove, which was also called the Lair of the White Worm. Such creatures may have grown down as well as up. They *may* have grown into, or something like, human beings. Lady Arabella March is of snake nature. She has committed crimes to our knowledge. She retains something of the vast strength of her primal being – can see in the dark – has the eyes of a snake. She used the African,* and then dragged him through the snake's hole down to the swamp; she is intent on evil, and hates some one we love. Result. . . "

"Yes, the result?"

"First, that Mimi Watford should be taken away at once – then – "

"Yes?"

"The monster must be destroyed."

"Bravo! That is a true and fearless conclusion. At whatever cost, it must be carried out."

"At once?"

"Soon, at all events. That creature's very existence is a danger. Her presence in this neighbourhood makes the danger immediate."

As he spoke, Sir Nathaniel's mouth hardened and his eyebrows came down till they met. There was no doubting his concurrence in the resolution, or his readiness to help in carrying it out. But he was an elderly man with much experience and knowledge of law and diplomacy. It seemed to him to be a stern duty to prevent anything irrevocable taking place till it had been thought out and all was ready. There were all sorts of legal cruxes to be thought out, not only regarding the taking of life, even of a monstrosity in human form, but also of property. Lady Arabella, be she woman or snake or devil, owned the ground she moved in, according to British law, and the law is jealous and swift to avenge wrongs done within its ken. All such difficulties should be – must be – avoided for Mr. Salton's sake, for Adam's own sake, and, most of all, for Mimi Watford's sake.

Before he spoke again, Sir Nathaniel had made up his mind that he must try to postpone decisive action until the circumstances on which they depended – which, after all, were only problematical – should have been tested satisfactorily, one way or another. When he did speak, Adam at first thought that his friend was wavering in his intention, or "funking" the responsibility. However, his respect for Sir Nathaniel was so great that he would not act, or even come to a conclusion on a vital point, without his sanction.

He came close and whispered in his ear:

"We will prepare our plans to combat and destroy this horrible menace, after we have cleared up some of the more baffling points. Meanwhile, we must wait for the night – I hear my uncle's footsteps echoing down the hall."

Sir Nathaniel nodded his approval.

CHAPTER XXI

GREEN LIGHT

WHEN OLD MR. SALTON HAD retired for the night, Adam and Sir Nathaniel returned to the study. Things went with great regularity at Lesser Hill, so they knew that there would be no interruption to their talk.

When their cigars were lighted, Sir Nathaniel began.

"I hope, Adam, that you do not think me either slack or changeable of purpose. I mean to go through this business to the bitter end – whatever it may be. Be satisfied that my first care is, and shall be, the protection of Mimi Watford. To that I am pledged; my dear boy, we who are interested are all in the same danger. That semi-human monster out of the pit hates and means to destroy us all – you and me certainly, and probably your uncle. I wanted especially to talk with you to-night, for I cannot help thinking that the time is fast coming – if it has not come already – when we must take your uncle into our confidence. It was one thing when fancied evils threatened, but now he is probably marked for death, and it is only right that he should know all."

"I am with you, sir. Things have changed since we agreed to keep him out of the trouble. Now we dare not; consideration for his feelings might cost his life. It is a duty – and no light or pleasant one, either. I have not a shadow of doubt that he will want to be one with us in this. But remember, we are his guests; his name, his honour, have to be thought of as well as his safety."

"All shall be as you wish, Adam. And now as to what we are to do? We cannot murder Lady Arabella off-hand. Therefore we shall have to put things in order for the killing, and in such a way that we cannot be taxed with a crime."

"It seems to me, sir, that we are in an exceedingly tight place. Our first difficulty is to know where to begin. I never thought this fighting an antediluvian monster would be such a complicated job. This one is a woman, with all a woman's wit, combined with the heartlessness of a *cocotte*. She has the strength and impregnability of a diplodocus. We may be sure that in the fight that is before us there will be no semblance of fair-play. Also that our unscrupulous opponent will not betray herself!"

"That is so – but being feminine, she will probably over-reach herself. Now, Adam, it strikes me that, as we have to protect our-

selves and others against feminine nature, our strong game will be
to play our masculine against her feminine. Perhaps we had better
sleep on it. She is a thing of the night; and the night may give us
some ideas."

So they both turned in.

Adam knocked at Sir Nathaniel's door in the grey of the morning, and, on being bidden, came into the room. He had several
letters in his hand. Sir Nathaniel sat up in bed.

"Well!"

"I should like to read you a few letters, but, of course, I shall
not send them unless you approve. In fact" – with a smile and a
blush – "there are several things which I want to do; but I hold
my hand and my tongue till I have your approval."

"Go on!" said the other kindly. "Tell me all, and count at any
rate on my sympathy, and on my approval and help if I can see
my way."

Accordingly Adam proceeded:

"When I told you the conclusions at which I had arrived, I put
in the foreground that Mimi Watford should, for the sake of her
own safety, be removed – and that the monster which had
wrought all the harm should be destroyed."

"Yes, that is so."

"To carry this into practice, sir, one preliminary is required –
unless harm of another kind is to be faced. Mimi should have
some protector whom all the world would recognise. The only
form recognised by convention is marriage!"

Sir Nathaniel smiled in a fatherly way.

"To marry, a husband is required. And that husband should be
you."

"Yes, yes."

"And the marriage should be immediate and secret – or, at least,
not spoken of outside ourselves. Would the young lady be agree-
able to that proceeding?"

"I do not know, sir!"

"Then how are we to proceed?"

"I suppose that we – or one of us – must ask her."

"Is this a sudden idea, Adam, a sudden resolution?"

"A sudden resolution, sir, but not a sudden idea. If she agrees,
all is well and good. The sequence is obvious."

"And it is to be kept a secret amongst ourselves?"

"I want no secret, sir, except for Mimi's good. For myself, I
should like to shout it from the house-tops! But we must be discreet; untimely knowledge to our enemy might work incalculable
harm."

"And how would you suggest, Adam, that we could combine
the momentous question with secrecy?"

Adam grew red and moved uneasily.

"Someone must ask her – as soon as possible!"

"And that someone?"

"I thought that you, sir, would be so good!"

"God bless my soul! This is a new kind of duty to take on – at my time of life. Adam, I hope you know that you can count on me to help in any way I can!"

"I have already counted on you, sir, when I ventured to make such a suggestion. I can only ask," he added, "that you will be more than ever kind to me – to us – and look on the painful duty as a voluntary act of grace, prompted by kindness and affection."

"Painful duty!"

"Yes," said Adam boldly. "Painful to you, though to me it would be all joyful."

"It is a strange job for an early morning! Well, we all live and learn. I suppose the sooner I go the better. You had better write a line for me to take with me. For, you see, this is to be a somewhat unusual transaction, and it may be embarrassing to the lady, even to myself. So we ought to have some sort of warrant, something to show that we have been mindful of her feelings. It will not do to take acquiescence for granted – although we act for her good."

"Sir Nathaniel, you are a true friend; I am sure that both Mimi and I shall be grateful to you for all our lives – however long they may be!"

So the two talked it over and agreed as to points to be borne in mind by the ambassador. It was striking ten when Sir Nathaniel left the house, Adam seeing him quietly off.

As the young man followed him with wistful eyes – almost jealous of the privilege which his kind deed was about to bring him – he felt that his own heart was in his friend's breast.

The memory of that morning was like a dream to all those concerned in it. Sir Nathaniel had a confused recollection of detail and sequence, though the main facts stood out in his memory boldly and clearly. Adam Salton's recollection was of an illimitable wait, filled with anxiety, hope, and chagrin, all dominated by a sense of the slow passage of time and accompanied by vague fears. Mimi could not for a long time think at all, or recollect anything, except that Adam loved her and was saving her from a terrible danger. When she had time to think, later on, she wondered when she had any ignorance of the fact that Adam loved her, and that she loved him with all her heart. Everything, every recollection however small, every feeling, seemed to fit into those elemental facts as though they had all been moulded together. The main and crowning recollection was her saying goodbye to Sir Nathaniel, and entrusting to him loving messages, straight from her heart, to Adam Salton, and of his bearing when – with an impulse which she could not check – she put her lips to his and kissed him. Later, when she was alone and had time to think, it was a passing grief to her that she would have to be silent, for a time, to Lilla on the happy events of that strange mission.

She had, of course, agreed to keep all secret until Adam should give her leave to speak.

The advice and assistance of Sir Nathaniel was a great help to Adam in carrying out his idea of marrying Mimi Watford without publicity. He went with him to London, and, with his influence, the young man obtained the license of the Archbishop of Canterbury for a private marriage. Sir Nathaniel then persuaded old Mr. Salton to allow his nephew to spend a few weeks with him at Doom Tower, and it was here that Mimi became Adam's wife. But that was only the first step in their plans; before going further, however, Adam took his bride off to the Isle of Man. He wished to place a stretch of sea between Mimi and the White Worm, while things matured. On their return, Sir Nathaniel met them and drove them at once to Doom, taking care to avoid any one that he knew on the journey.

Sir Nathaniel had taken care to have the doors and windows shut and locked – all but the door used for their entry. The shutters were up and the blinds down. Moreover, heavy curtains were drawn across the windows. When Adam commented on this, Sir Nathaniel said in a whisper:

"Wait till we are alone, and I'll tell you why this is done; in the meantime not a word or a sign. You will approve when we have had a talk together."

They said no more on the subject till after dinner, when they were ensconced in Sir Nathaniel's study, which was on the top storey. Doom Tower was a lofty structure, situated on an eminence high up in the Peak. The top commanded a wide prospect, ranging from the hills above the Ribble to the near side of the Brow, which marked the northern bound of ancient Mercia. It was of the early Norman period, less than a century younger than Castra Regis. The windows of the study were barred and locked, and heavy dark curtains closed them in. When this was done not a gleam of light from the tower could be seen from outside.

When they were alone, Sir Nathaniel explained that he had taken his old friend, Mr. Salton, into full confidence, and that in future all would work together.

"It is important for you to be extremely careful. In spite of the fact that our marriage was kept secret, as also your temporary absence, both are known."

"How? To whom?"

"How, I know not; but I am beginning to have an idea."

"To her?" asked Adam, in momentary consternation.

Sir Nathaniel shivered perceptibly.

"The White Worm – yes!"

Adam noticed that from now on, his friend never spoke of Lady Arabella otherwise, except when he wished to divert the suspicion of others.

Sir Nathaniel switched off the electric light, and when the room was pitch dark, he came to Adam, took him by the hand, and led him to a seat set in the southern window. Then he softly drew back a piece of the curtain and motioned his companion to look out.

Adam did so, and immediately shrank back as though his eyes had opened on pressing danger. His companion set his mind at rest by saying in a low voice:

"It is all right; you may speak, but speak low. There is no danger here – at present!"

Adam leaned forward, taking care, however, not to press his face against the glass. What he saw would not under ordinary circumstances have caused concern to anybody. With his special knowledge, it was appalling – though the night was now so dark that in reality there was little to be seen.

On the western side of the tower stood a grove of old trees, of forest dimensions. They were not grouped closely, but stood a little apart from each other, producing the effect of a row widely planted. Over the tops of them was seen a green light, something like the danger signal at a railway-crossing. It seemed at first quite still; but presently, when Adam's eye became accustomed to it, he could see that it moved as if trembling. This at once recalled to Adam's mind the light quivering above the well-hole in the darkness of that inner room at Diana's Grove, Oolanga's awful shriek, and the hideous black face, now grown grey with terror, disappearing into the impenetrable gloom of the mysterious orifice. Instinctively he laid his hand on his revolver, and stood up ready to protect his wife. Then, seeing that nothing happened, and that the light and all outside the tower remained the same, he softly pulled the curtain over the window.

Sir Nathaniel switched on the light again, and in its comforting glow they began to talk freely.

CHAPTER XXII
AT CLOSE QUARTERS

"SHE HAS DIABOLICAL CUNNING," said Sir Nathaniel. "Ever since you left, she has ranged along the Brow and wherever you were accustomed to frequent. I have not heard whence the knowledge of your movements came to her, nor have I been able to learn any data whereon to found an opinion. She seems to have heard both of your marriage and your absence; but I gather, by inference, that she does not actually know where you and Mimi are, or of your return. So soon as the dusk fails, she goes out on her rounds, and before dawn covers the whole ground round the Brow, and away up into the heart of the Peak. The White Worm, in her own proper shape, certainly has great facilities for the business on which she is now engaged. She can look into windows of any ordinary kind. Happily, this house is beyond her reach, if she wishes – as she manifestly does – to remain unrecognised. But, even at this height, it is wise to show no lights, lest she might learn something of our presence or absence."

"Would it not be well, sir, if one of us could see this monster in her real shape at close quarters? I am willing to run the risk – for I take it there would be no slight risk in the doing. I don't suppose anyone of our time has seen her close and lived to tell the tale."

Sir Nathaniel held up an expostulatory hand.

"Good God, lad, what are you suggesting? Think of your wife, and all that is at stake."

"It is of Mimi that I think – for her sake that I am willing to risk whatever is to be risked."

Adam's young bride was proud of her man, but she blanched at the thought of the ghastly White Worm. Adam saw this and at once reassured her.

"So long as her ladyship does not know whereabout I am, I shall have as much safety as remains to us; bear in mind, my darling, that we cannot be too careful."

Sir Nathaniel realised that Adam was right; the White Worm had no supernatural powers and could not harm them until she discovered their hiding place. It was agreed, therefore, that the two men should go together.

When the two men slipped out by the back door of the house, they walked cautiously along the avenue which trended towards the west. Everything was pitch dark – so dark that at times they had to feel their way by the palings and tree-trunks. They could still see, seemingly far in front of them and high up, the baleful light which at the height and distance seemed like a faint line. As they were now on the level of the ground, the light seemed infinitely higher than it had from the top of the tower. At the sight Adam's heart fell; the danger of the desperate enterprise which he had undertaken burst upon him. But this feeling was shortly followed by another which restored him to himself – a fierce loathing, and a desire to kill, such as he had never experienced before.

They went on for some distance on a level road, fairly wide, from which the green light was visible. Here Sir Nathaniel spoke softly, placing his lips to Adam's ear for safety.

"We know nothing whatever of this creature's power of hearing or smelling, though I presume that both are of no great strength. As to seeing, we may presume the opposite, but in any case we must try to keep in the shade behind the tree-trunks. The slightest error would be fatal to us."

Adam only nodded, in case there should be any chance of the monster seeing the movement.

After a time that seemed interminable, they emerged from the circling wood. It was like coming out into sunlight by comparison with the misty blackness which had been around them. There was light enough to see by, though not sufficient to distinguish things at a distance. Adam's eyes sought the green light in the sky. It was still in about the same place, but its surroundings were more visible. It was now at the summit of what seemed to be a long white pole, near the top of which were two pendant white masses, like rudimentary arms or fins. The green light, strangely enough, did not seem lessened by the surrounding starlight, but had a clearer effect and a deeper green. Whilst they were carefully regarding this – Adam with the aid of an opera-glass – their nostrils were assailed by a horrid stench, something like that which rose from the well-hole in Diana's Grove.

By degrees, as their eyes got the right focus, they saw an immense towering mass that seemed snowy white. It was tall and thin. The lower part was hidden by the trees which lay between, but they could follow the tall white shaft and the duplicate green lights which topped it. As they looked there was a movement – the shaft seemed to bend, and the line of green light descended amongst the trees. They could see the green light twinkle as it passed between the obstructing branches.

Seeing where the head of the monster was, the two men ventured a little further forward, and saw that the hidden mass at the base of the shaft was composed of vast coils of the great serpent's body, forming a base from which the upright mass rose. As they looked, this lower mass moved, the glistening folds catching the moonlight, and they could see that the monster's progress was along the ground. It was coming towards them at a swift pace, so they turned and ran, taking care to make as little noise as possible, either by their footfalls or by disturbing the undergrowth close to them. They did not stop or pause till they saw before them the high dark tower of Doom.

CHAPTER XXIII

IN THE ENEMY'S HOUSE

SIR NATHANIEL WAS IN THE library next morning, after breakfast, when Adam came to him carrying a letter.

"Her ladyship doesn't lose any time. She has begun work already!"

Sir Nathaniel, who was writing at a table near the window, looked up.

"What is it?" said he.

Adam held out the letter he was carrying. It was in a blazoned envelope.

"Ha!" said Sir Nathaniel, "from the White Worm! I expected something of the kind."

"But," said Adam, "how could she have known we were here? She didn't know last night."

"I don't think we need trouble about that, Adam. There is so much we do not understand. This is only another mystery. Suffice it that she does know – perhaps it is all the better and safer for us."

"How is that?" asked Adam with a puzzled look.

"General process of reasoning, my boy; and the experience of some years in the diplomatic world. This creature is a monster without heart or consideration for anything or anyone. She is not nearly so dangerous in the open as when she has the dark to protect her. Besides, we know, by our own experience of her movements, that for some reason she shuns publicity. In spite of her vast bulk and abnormal strength, she is afraid to attack openly. After all, she is only a snake and with a snake's nature, which is to keep low and squirm, and proceed by stealth and cunning. She will never attack when she can run away, although she knows well that running away would probably be fatal to her. What is the letter about?"

Sir Nathaniel's voice was calm and self-possessed. When he was engaged in any struggle of wits he was all diplomatist.

"She asks Mimi and me to tea this afternoon at Diana's Grove, and hopes that you also will favour her."

Sir Nathaniel smiled.

"Please ask Mrs. Salton to accept for us all."

"She means some deadly mischief. Surely – surely it would be wiser not."

"It is an old trick that we learn early in diplomacy, Adam – to fight on ground of your own choice. It is true that she suggested the place on this occasion; but by accepting it we make it ours. Moreover, she will not be able to understand our reason for doing so, and her own bad conscience – if she has any, bad or good – and her own fears and doubts will play our game for us. No, my dear boy, let us accept, by all means."

Adam said nothing, but silently held out his hand, which his companion shook: no words were necessary.

When it was getting near tea-time, Mimi asked Sir Nathaniel how they were going.

"We must make a point of going in state. We want all possible publicity." Mimi looked at him inquiringly. "Certainly, my dear, in the present circumstances publicity is a part of safety. Do not be surprised if, whilst we are at Diana's Grove, occasional messages come for you – for all or any of us."

"I see!" said Mrs. Salton. "You are taking no chances."

"None, my dear. All I have learned at foreign courts, and amongst civilised and uncivilised people, is going to be utilised within the next couple of hours."

Sir Nathaniel's voice was full of seriousness, and it brought to Mimi in a convincing way the awful gravity of the occasion

In due course, they set out in a carriage drawn by a fine pair of horses, who soon devoured the few miles of their journey. Before they came to the gate, Sir Nathaniel turned to Mimi.

"I have arranged with Adam certain signals which may be necessary if certain eventualities occur. These need be nothing to do with you directly. But bear in mind that if I ask you or Adam to do anything, do not lose a second in the doing of it. We must try to pass off such moments with an appearance of unconcern. In all probability, nothing requiring such care will occur. The White Worm will not try force, though she has so much of it to spare. Whatever she may attempt to-day, of harm to any of us, will be in the way of secret plot. Some other time she may try force, but – if I am able to judge such a thing – not to-day. The messengers who may ask for any of us will not be witnesses only, they may help to stave off danger." Seeing query in her face, he went on: "Of what kind the danger may be, I know not, and cannot guess. It will doubtless be some ordinary circumstance; but none the less dangerous on that account. Here we are at the gate. Now, be careful in all matters, however small. To keep your head is half the battle."

There were a number of men in livery in the hall when they arrived. The doors of the drawing-room were thrown open, and Lady Arabella came forth and offered them cordial welcome. This having been got over, Lady Arabella led them into another room where tea was served.

Adam was acutely watchful and suspicious of everything, and saw on the far side of this room a panelled iron door of the same colour and configuration as the outer door of the room where was the well-hole wherein Oolanga had disappeared. Something in the sight alarmed him, and he quietly stood near the door. He made no movement, even of his eyes, but he could see that Sir Nathaniel was watching him intently, and, he fancied, with approval.

They all sat near the table spread for tea, Adam still near the door. Lady Arabella fanned herself, complaining of heat, and told one of the footmen to throw all the outer doors open.

Tea was in progress when Mimi suddenly started up with a look of fright on her face; at the same moment, the men became cognisant of a thick smoke which began to spread through the room – a smoke which made those who experienced it gasp and choke. The footmen began to edge uneasily towards the inner door. Denser and denser grew the smoke, and more acrid its smell. Mimi, towards whom the draught from the open door wafted the smoke, rose up choking, and ran to the inner door, which she threw open to its fullest extent, disclosing on the outside a curtain of thin silk, fixed to the doorposts. The draught from the open door swayed the thin silk towards her, and in her fright, she tore down the curtain, which enveloped her from head to foot. Then she ran through the still open door, heedless of the fact that she could not see where she was going. Adam, followed by Sir Nathaniel, rushed forward and joined her – Adam catching his wife by the arm and holding her tight. It was well that he did so, for just before her lay the black orifice of the well-hole, which, of course, she could not see with the silk curtain round her head. The floor was extremely slippery; something like thick oil had been spilled where she had to pass; and close to the edge of the hole her feet shot from under her, and she stumbled forward towards the well-hole.

When Adam saw Mimi slip, he flung himself backward, still holding her. His weight told, and he dragged her up from the hole and they fell together on the floor outside the zone of slipperiness. In a moment he had raised her up, and together they rushed out through the open door into the sunlight, Sir Nathaniel close behind them. They were all pale except the old diplomatist, who looked both calm and cool. It sustained and cheered Adam and his wife to see him thus master of himself. Both managed to follow his example, to the wonderment of the footmen, who saw the three who had just escaped a terrible danger walking together gaily as, under the guiding pressure of Sir Nathaniel's hand, they turned to re-enter the house.

Lady Arabella, whose face had blanched to a deadly white, now resumed her ministrations at the tea-board as though nothing unusual had happened. The slop-basin was full of half-burned brown paper, over which tea had been poured.

Sir Nathaniel had been narrowly observing his hostess, and took the first opportunity afforded him of whispering to Adam:

"The real attack is to come – she is too quiet. When I give my hand to your wife to lead her out, come with us – and caution her to hurry. Don't lose a second, even if you have to make a scene. Hs-s-s-h!"

Then they resumed their places close to the table, and the servants, in obedience to Lady Arabella's order, brought in fresh tea.

Thence on, that tea-party seemed to Adam, whose faculties were at their utmost intensity, like a terrible dream. As for poor Mimi, she was so overwrought both with present and future fear, and with horror at the danger she had escaped, that her faculties were numb. However, she was braced up for a trial, and she felt assured that whatever might come she would be able to go through with it. Sir Nathaniel seemed just as usual – suave, digni-fied, and thoughtful – perfect master of himself.

To her husband, it was evident that Mimi was ill at ease. The way she kept turning her head to look around her, the quick com-ing and going of the colour of her face, her hurried breathing, alternating with periods of suspicious calm, were evidences of mental perturbation. To her, the attitude of Lady Arabella seemed compounded of social sweetness and personal consideration. It would be hard to imagine more thoughtful and tender kindness towards an honoured guest.

When tea was over and the servants had come to clear away the cups, Lady Arabella, putting her arm round Mimi's waist, strolled with her into an adjoining room, where she collected a number of photographs which were scattered about, and, sitting down beside her guest, began to show them to her. While she was doing this, the servants closed all the doors of the suite of rooms, as well as that which opened from the room outside – that of the well-hole into the avenue. Suddenly, without any seeming cause, the light in the room began to grow dim. Sir Nathaniel, who was sitting close to Mimi, rose to his feet, and, crying, "Quick!" caught hold of her hand and began to drag her from the room. Adam caught her other hand, and between them they drew her through the outer door which the servants were beginning to close. It was difficult at first to find the way, the darkness was so great; but to their re-lief when Adam whistled shrilly, the carriage and horses, which had been waiting in the angle of the avenue, dashed up. Her hus-band and Sir Nathaniel lifted – almost threw – Mimi into the car-riage. The postillion plied whip and spur, and the vehicle, rocking with its speed, swept through the gate and tore up the road. Be-hind them was a hubbub – servants rushing about, orders being shouted out, doors shutting, and somewhere, seemingly far back in the house, a strange noise. Every nerve of the horses was strained as they dashed recklessly along the road. The two men held Mimi between them, the arms of both of them round her as though protectingly. As they went, there was a sudden rise in the ground; but the horses, breathing heavily, dashed up it at racing speed, not slackening their pace when the hill fell away again, leav-ing them to hurry along the downgrade.

It would be foolish to say that neither Adam nor Mimi had any fear in returning to Doom Tower. Mimi felt it more keenly than her husband, whose nerves were harder, and who was more inured to danger. Still she bore up bravely, and as usual the effort was helpful to her. When once she was in the study in the top of the turret, she almost forgot the terrors which lay outside in the dark. She did not attempt to peep out of the window; but Adam did – and saw nothing. The moonlight showed all the surrounding country, but nowhere was to be observed that tremulous line of green light.

The peaceful night had a good effect on them all; danger, being unseen, seemed far off. At times it was hard to realise that it had ever been. With courage restored, Adam rose early and walked along the Brow, seeing no change in the signs of life in Castra Regis. What he did see, to his wonder and concern, on his returning homeward, was Lady Arabella, in her tight-fitting white dress and ermine collar, but without her emeralds; she was emerging from the gate of Diana's Grove and walking towards the Castle. Pondering on this and trying to find some meaning in it, occupied his thoughts till he joined Mimi and Sir Nathaniel at breakfast. They began the meal in silence. What had been had been, and was known to them all. Moreover, it was not a pleasant topic.

A fillip was given to the conversation when Adam told of his seeing Lady Arabella, on her way to Castra Regis. They each had something to say of her, and of what her wishes or intentions were towards Edgar Caswall. Mimi spoke bitterly of her in every aspect. She had not forgotten – and never would – never could – the occasion when, to harm Lilla, the woman had consorted even with the African.* As a social matter, she was disgusted with her for following up the rich landowner – "throwing herself at his head so shamelessly," was how she expressed it. She was interested to know that the great kite still flew from Caswall's tower. But beyond such matters she did not try to go. The only comment she made was of strongly expressed surprise at her ladyship's "cheek" in ignoring her own criminal acts, and her impudence in taking it for granted that others had overlooked them also.

CHAPTER XXIV

A STARTLING PROPOSITION

THE MORE MIMI THOUGHT over the late events, the more puzzled she was. What did it all mean – what could it mean, except that there was an error of fact somewhere. Could it be possible that some of them – all of them had been mistaken, that there had been no White Worm at all? On either side of her was a belief impossible of reception. Not to believe in what seemed apparent was to destroy the very foundations of belief. . . yet in old days there had been monsters on the earth, and certainly some people had believed in just such mysterious changes of identity. It was all very strange. Just fancy how any stranger – say a doctor – would regard her, if she were to tell him that she had been to a tea-party with an antediluvian monster, and that they had been waited on by up-to-date men-servants.

Adam had returned, exhilarated by his walk, and more settled in his mind than he had been for some time. Like Mimi, he had gone through the phase of doubt and inability to believe in the reality of things, though it had not affected him to the same extent. The idea, however, that his wife was suffering ill-effects from her terrible ordeal, braced him up. He remained with her for a time, then he sought Sir Nathaniel in order to talk over the matter with him. He knew that the calm common sense and self-reliance of the old man, as well as his experience, would be helpful to them all.

Sir Nathaniel had come to the conclusion that, for some reason which he did not understand, Lady Arabella had changed her plans, and, for the present at all events, was pacific. He was inclined to attribute her changed demeanour to the fact that her influence over Edgar Caswall was so far increased, as to justify a more fixed belief in his submission to her charms.

As a matter of fact, she had seen Caswall that morning when she visited Castra Regis, and they had had a long talk together, during which the possibility of their union had been discussed. Caswall, without being enthusiastic on the subject, had been courteous and attentive; as she had walked back to Diana's Grove, she almost congratulated herself on her new settlement in life. That the idea was becoming fixed in her mind, was shown by a letter which she wrote later in the day to Adam Salton, and sent to him by hand. It ran as follows:

"*Dear Mr. Salton,*

"I wonder if you would kindly advise, and, if possible, help me in a matter of business. I have been for some time trying to make up my mind to sell Diana's Grove, I have put off and put off the doing of it till now. The place is my own property, and no one has to be consulted with regard to what I may wish to do about it. It was bought by my late husband, Captain Adolphus Ranger March, who had another residence, The Crest, Appleby. He acquired all rights of all kinds, including mining and sporting. When he died, he left his whole property to me. I shall feel leaving this place, which has become endeared to me by many sacred memories and affections – the recollection of many happy days of my young married life, and the more than happy memories of the man I loved and who loved me so much. I should be willing to sell the place for any fair price – so long, of course, as the purchaser was one I liked and of whom I approved. May I say that you yourself would be the ideal person. But I dare not hope for so much. It strikes me, however, that among your Australian friends may be someone who wishes to make a settlement in the Old Country, and would care to fix the spot in one of the most historic regions in England, full of romance and legend, and with a never-ending vista of historical interest – an estate which, though small, is in perfect condition and with illimitable possibilities of development, and many doubtful – or unsettled – rights which have existed before the time of the Romans or even Celts, who were the original possessors. In addition, the house has been kept up to the *dernier cri*. Immediate possession can be arranged. My lawyers can provide you, or whoever you may suggest, with all business and historical details. A word from you of acceptance or refusal is all that is necessary, and we can leave details to be thrashed out by our agents. Forgive me, won't you, for troubling you in the matter, and believe me, yours very sincerely.

"*Arabella March.*"

Adam read this over several times, and then, his mind being made up, he went to Mimi and asked if she had any objection. She answered – after a shudder – that she was, in this, as in all things, willing to do whatever he might wish.

"Dearest, I am willing that you should judge what is best for us. Be quite free to act as you see your duty, and as your inclination calls. We are in the hands of God, and He has hitherto guided us, and will do so to His own end."

From his wife's room Adam Salton went straight to the study in the tower, where he knew Sir Nathaniel would be at that hour. The old man was alone, so, when he had entered in obedience to the "Come in," which answered his query, he closed the door and sat down beside him.

"Do you think, sir, that it would be well for me to buy Diana's Grove?"

"God bless my soul!" said the old man, startled, "why on earth would you want to do that?"

"Well, I have vowed to destroy that White Worm, and my being able to do whatever I may choose with the Lair would facilitate matters and avoid complications."

Sir Nathaniel hesitated longer than usual before speaking. He was thinking deeply.

"Yes, Adam, there is much common sense in your suggestion, though it startled me at first. I think that, for all reasons, you would do well to buy the property and to have the conveyance settled at once. If you want more money than is immediately convenient, let me know, so that I may be your banker."

"Thank you, sir, most heartily; but I have more money at immediate call than I shall want. I am glad you approve."

"The property is historic, and as time goes on it will increase in value. Moreover, I may tell you something, which indeed is only a surmise, but which, if I am right, will add great value to the place." Adam listened. "Has it ever struck you why the old name, 'The Lair of the White Worm,' was given? We know that there was a snake which in early days was called a worm; but why white?"

"I really don't know, sir; I never thought of it. I simply took it for granted."

"So did I at first – long ago. But later I puzzled my brain for a reason."

"And what was the reason, sir?"

"Simply and solely because the snake or worm *was* white. We are near the county of Stafford, where the great industry of china-burning was originated and grew. Stafford owes much of its wealth to the large deposits of the rare china clay found in it from time to time. These deposits become in time pretty well exhausted; but for centuries Stafford adventurers looked for the special clay, as Ohio and Pennsylvania farmers and explorers looked for oil. Anyone owning real estate on which china clay can be discovered strikes a sort of gold mine."

"Yes, and then – " The young man looked puzzled.

"The original 'Worm' so-called, from which the name of the place came, had to find a direct way down to the marshes and the mud-holes. Now, the clay is easily penetrable, and the original hole probably pierced a bed of china clay. When once the way was made it would become a sort of highway for the Worm. But as much movement was necessary to ascend such a great height, some of the clay would become attached to its rough skin by attrition. The downway must have been easy work, but the ascent was different, and when the monster came to view in the upper world, it would be fresh from contact with the white clay. Hence the name, which has no cryptic significance, but only fact. Now, if that surmise be true – and I do not see why not – there must be a deposit of valuable clay – possibly of immense depth."

Adam's comment pleased the old gentleman.

"I have it in my bones, sir, that you have struck – or rather reasoned out – a great truth."

Sir Nathaniel went on cheerfully. "When the world of commerce wakes up to the value of your find, it will be as well that your title to ownership has been perfectly secured. If anyone ever deserved such a gain, it is you."

With his friend's aid, Adam secured the property without loss of time. Then he went to see his uncle, and told him about it. Mr. Salton was delighted to find his young relative already constructively the owner of so fine an estate – one which gave him an important status in the county. He made many anxious enquiries about Mimi, and the doings of the White Worm, but Adam reassured him.

The next morning, when Adam went to his host in the smoking-room, Sir Nathaniel asked him how he purposed to proceed with regard to keeping his vow.

"It is a difficult matter which you have undertaken. To destroy such a monster is something like one of the labours of Hercules, in that not only its size and weight and power of using them in little-known ways are against you, but the occult side is alone an unsurpassable difficulty. The Worm is already master of all the elements except fire – and I do not see how fire can be used for the attack. It has only to sink into the earth in its usual way, and you could not overtake it if you had the resources of the biggest coal-mine in existence. But I daresay you have mapped out some plan in your mind," he added courteously.

"I have, sir. But, of course, it may not stand the test of practice."

"May I know the idea?"

"Well, sir, this was my argument: At the time of the Chartist trouble, an idea spread amongst financial circles that an attack was going to be made on the Bank of England. Accordingly, the directors of that institution consulted many persons who were supposed to know what steps should be taken, and it was finally decided that the best protection against fire – which is what was feared – was not water but sand. To carry the scheme into practice great store of fine sea-sand – the kind that blows about and is used to fill hour-glasses – was provided throughout the building, especially at the points liable to attack, from which it could be brought into use.

"I propose to provide at Diana's Grove, as soon as it comes into my possession, an enormous amount of such sand, and shall take an early occasion of pouring it into the well-hole, which it will in time choke. Thus Lady Arabella, in her guise of the White Worm, will find herself cut off from her refuge. The hole is a narrow one, and is some hundreds of feet deep. The weight of the sand this can contain would not in itself be sufficient to obstruct; but the friction of such a body working up against it would be tremendous."

"One moment. What use would the sand be for destruction?"

"None, directly; but it would hold the struggling body in place till the rest of my scheme came into practice."

"And what is the rest?"

"As the sand is being poured into the well-hole, quantities of dynamite can also be thrown in!"

"Good. But how would the dynamite explode – for, of course,

that is what you intend. Would not some sort of wire or fuse he required for each parcel of dynamite?"

Adam smiled.

"Not in these days, sir. That was proved in New York. A thousand pounds of dynamite, in sealed canisters, was placed about some workings. At the last a charge of gunpowder was fired, and the concussion exploded the dynamite. It was most successful. Those who were non-experts in high explosives expected that every pane of glass in New York would be shattered. But, in reality, the explosive did no harm outside the area intended, although sixteen acres of rock had been mined and only the supporting walls and pillars had been left intact. The whole of the rocks were shattered."

Sir Nathaniel nodded approval.

"That seems a good plan – a very excellent one. But if it has to tear down so many feet of precipice, it may wreck the whole neighbourhood."

"And free it for ever from a monster," added Adam, as he left the room to find his wife.

CHAPTER XXV

THE LAST BATTLE

LADY ARABELLA HAD INSTRUCTED her solicitors to hurry on with the conveyance of Diana's Grove, so no time was lost in letting Adam Salton have formal possession of the estate. After his interview with Sir Nathaniel, he had taken steps to begin putting his plan into action. In order to accumulate the necessary amount of fine sea-sand, he ordered the steward to prepare for an elaborate system of top-dressing all the grounds. A great heap of the sand, brought from bays on the Welsh coast, began to grow at the back of the Grove. No one seemed to suspect that it was there for any purpose other than what had been given out.

Lady Arabella, who alone could have guessed, was now so absorbed in her matrimonial pursuit of Edgar Caswall, that she had neither time nor inclination for thought extraneous to this. She had not yet moved from the house, though she had formally handed over the estate.

Adam put up a rough corrugated-iron shed behind the Grove, in which he stored his explosives. All being ready for his great attempt whenever the time should come, he was now content to wait, and, in order to pass the time, interested himself in other things – even in Caswall's great kite, which still flew from the high tower of Castra Regis.

The mound of fine sand grew to proportions so vast as to puzzle the bailiffs and farmers round the Brow. The hour of the intended cataclysm was approaching apace. Adam wished – but in vain – for an opportunity, which would appear to be natural, of visiting Caswall in the turret of Castra Regis. At last, one morning, he met Lady Arabella moving towards the Castle, so he took his courage *e deux mains* and asked to be allowed to accompany her. She was glad, for her own purposes, to comply with his wishes. So together they entered, and found their way to the turret-room. Caswall was much surprised to see Adam come to his house, but lent himself to the task of seeming to be pleased. He played the host so well as to deceive even Adam. They all went out on the turret roof, where he explained to his guests the mechanism for raising and lowering the kite, taking also the opportunity of testing the movements of the multitudes of birds, how they answered almost instantaneously to the lowering or raising of the kite.

As Lady Arabella walked home with Adam from Castra Regis, she asked him if she might make a request. Permission having been accorded, she explained that before she finally left Diana's Grove, where she had lived so long, she had a desire to know the depth of the well-hole. Adam was really happy to meet her wishes, not from any sentiment, but because he wished to give some valid and ostensible reason for examining the passage of the Worm, which would obviate any suspicion resulting from his being on the premises. He brought from London a Kelvin sounding apparatus, with a sufficient length of piano-wire for testing any probable depth. The wire passed easily over the running wheel, and when this was once fixed over the hole, he was satisfied to wait till the most advantageous time for his final experiment.

In the meantime, affairs had been going quietly at Mercy Farm. Lilla, of course, felt lonely in the absence of her cousin, but the even tenor of life went on for her as for others. After the first shock of parting was over, things went back to their accustomed routine. In one respect, however, there was a marked difference. So long as home conditions had remained unchanged, Lilla was content to put ambition far from her, and to settle down to the life which had been hers as long as she could remember. But Mimi's marriage set her thinking; naturally, she came to the conclusion that she too might have a mate. There was not for her much choice – there was little movement in the matrimonial direction at the farmhouse. She did not approve of the personality of Edgar Caswall, and his struggle with Mimi had frightened her; but he was unmistakably an excellent *parti*, much better than she could have any right to expect. This weighs much with a woman, and more particularly one of her class. So, on the whole, she was content to let things take their course, and to abide by the issue.

As time went on, she had reason to believe that things did not point to happiness. She could not shut her eyes to certain disturbing facts, amongst which were the existence of Lady Arabella and her growing intimacy with Edgar Caswall; as well as his own cold and haughty nature, so little in accord with the ardour which is the foundation of a young maid's dreams of happiness. How things would, of necessity, alter if she were to marry, she was afraid to think. All told, the prospect was not happy for her, and she had a secret longing that something might occur to upset the order of things as at present arranged.

When Lilla received a note from Edgar Caswall asking if he might come to tea on the following afternoon, her heart sank within her. If it was only for her father's sake, she must not refuse him or show any disinclination which he might construe into incivility. She missed Mimi more than she could say or even dared to think. Hitherto, she had always looked to her cousin for sympathy, for understanding, for loyal support. Now she and all these things, and a thousand others – gentle, assuring, supporting – were gone. And instead there was a horrible aching void.

For the whole afternoon and evening, and for the following forenoon, poor Lilla's loneliness grew to be a positive agony. For the first time she began to realise the sense of her loss, as though all the previous suffering had been merely a preparation. Everything she looked at, everything she remembered or thought of, became laden with poignant memory. Then on the top of all was a new sense of dread. The reaction from the sense of security, which had surrounded her all her life, to a never-quieted apprehension, was at times almost more than she could bear. It so filled her with fear that she had a haunting feeling that she would as soon die as live. However, whatever might be her own feelings, duty had to be done, and as she had been brought up to consider duty first, she braced herself to go through, to the very best of her ability, what was before her.

Still, the severe and prolonged struggle for self-control told upon Lilla. She looked, as she felt, ill and weak. She was really in a nerveless and prostrate condition, with black circles round her eyes, pale even to her lips, and with an instinctive trembling which she was quite unable to repress. It was for her a sad mischance that Mimi was away, for her love would have seen through all obscuring causes, and have brought to light the girl's unhappy condition of health. Lilla was utterly unable to do anything to escape from the ordeal before her; but her cousin, with the experience of her former struggles with Mr. Caswall and of the condition in which these left her, would have taken steps – even peremptory ones, if necessary – to prevent a repetition.

Edgar arrived punctually to the time appointed by herself. When Lilla, through the great window, saw him approaching the house, her condition of nervous upset was pitiable. She braced herself up, however, and managed to get through the interview in its preliminary stages without any perceptible change in her normal appearance and bearing. It had been to her an added terror that the black shadow of Oolanga, whom she dreaded, would follow hard on his master. A load was lifted from her mind when he did not make his usual stealthy approach. She had also feared, though in lesser degree, lest Lady Arabella should be present to make trouble for her as before.

With a woman's natural forethought in a difficult position, she had provided the furnishing of the tea-table as a subtle indication of the social difference between her and her guest. She had chosen the implements of service, as well as all the provender set forth, of the humblest kind. Instead of arranging the silver teapot and china cups, she had set out an earthen tea-pot, such as was in common use in the farm kitchen. The same idea was carried out in the cups and saucers of thick homely delft, and in the cream-jug of similar kind. The bread was of simple whole-meal, home-baked. The butter was good, since she had made it herself, while the preserves and honey came from her own garden. Her face beamed with satisfaction when the guest eyed the appointments with a supercilious glance. It was a shock to the poor girl herself, for she enjoyed offering to a guest the little hospitalities possible to her; but that had to be sacrificed with other pleasures.

Caswall's face was more set and iron-clad than ever – his piercing eyes seemed from the very beginning to look her through and through. Her heart quailed when she thought of what would follow – of what would be the end, when this was only the beginning. As some protection, though it could be only of a sentimental kind, she brought from her own room the photographs of Mimi, of her grandfather, and of Adam Salton, whom by now she had grown to look on with reliance, as a brother whom she could trust. She kept the pictures near her heart, to which her hand naturally strayed when her feelings of constraint, distrust, or fear became so poignant as to interfere with the calm which she felt was necessary to help her through her ordeal.

At first Edgar Caswall was courteous and polite, even thoughtful; but after a little while, when he found her resistance to his domination grow, he abandoned all forms of self-control and appeared in the same dominance as he had previously shown. She was prepared, however, for this, both by her former experience and the natural fighting instinct within her. By this means, as the minutes went on, both developed the power and preserved the equality in which they had begun.

Without warning, the psychic battle between the two individualities began afresh. This time both the positive and negative causes were all in favour of the man. The woman was alone and in bad spirits, unsupported; nothing at all was in her favour except the memory of the two victorious contests; whereas the man, though unaided, as before, by either Lady Arabella or Oolanga, was in full strength, well rested, and in flourishing circumstances. It was not, therefore, to be wondered at that his native dominance of character had full opportunity of asserting itself. He began his preliminary stare with a conscious sense of power, and, as it appeared to have immediate effect on the girl, he felt an ever-growing conviction of ultimate victory.

After a little Lilla's resolution began to flag. She felt that the contest was unequal – that she was unable to put forth her best efforts. As she was an unselfish person, she could not fight so well in her own battle as in that of someone whom she loved and to whom she was devoted. Edgar saw the relaxing of the muscles of face and brow, and the almost collapse of the heavy eyelids which seemed tumbling downward in sleep. Lilla made gallant efforts to brace her dwindling powers, but for a time unsuccessfully. At length there came an interruption, which seemed like a powerful stimulant. Through the wide window she saw Lady Arabella enter the plain gateway of the farm, and advance towards the hall door. She was clad as usual in tight-fitting white, which accentuated her thin, sinuous figure.

The sight did for Lilla what no voluntary effort could have done. Her eyes flashed, and in an instant she felt as though a new life had suddenly developed within her. Lady Arabella's entry, in her usual unconcerned, haughty, supercilious way, heightened the effect, so that when the two stood close to each other battle was joined. Mr. Caswall, too, took new courage from her coming, and all his masterfulness and power came back to him. His looks, intensified, had more obvious effect than had been noticeable that day. Lilla seemed at last overcome by his dominance. Her face became red and pale – violently red and ghastly pale – by rapid turns. Her strength seemed gone. Her knees collapsed, and she was actually sinking on the floor, when to her surprise and joy Mimi came into the room, running hurriedly and breathing heavily.

Lilla rushed to her, and the two clasped hands. With that, a new sense of power, greater than Lilla had ever seen in her, seemed to quicken her cousin. Her hand swept the air in front of Edgar Caswall, seeming to drive him backward more and more by each movement, till at last he seemed to be actually hurled through the door which Mimi's entrance had left open, and fell at full length on the gravel path without.

Then came the final and complete collapse of Lilla, who, without a sound, sank down on the floor.

CHAPTER XXVI
FACE TO FACE

MIMI WAS GREATLY DISTRESSED when she saw her cousin lying prone. She had a few times in her life seen Lilla on the verge of fainting, but never senseless; and now she was frightened. She threw herself on her knees beside Lilla, and tried, by rubbing her hands and other measures commonly known, to restore her. But all her efforts were unavailing. Lilla still lay white and senseless. In fact, each moment she looked worse; her breast, that had been heaving with the stress, became still, and the pallor of her face grew like marble.

At these succeeding changes Mimi's fright grew, till it altogether mastered her. She succeeded in controlling herself only to the extent that she did not scream.

Lady Arabella had followed Caswall, when he had recovered sufficiently to get up and walk – though stumblingly – in the direction of Castra Regis. When Mimi was quite alone with Lilla and the need for effort had ceased, she felt weak and trembled. In her own mind, she attributed it to a sudden change in the weather – it was momentarily becoming apparent that a storm was coming on.

She raised Lilla's head and laid it on her warm young breast, but all in vain. The cold of the white features thrilled through her, and she utterly collapsed when it was borne in on her that Lilla had passed away.

The dusk gradually deepened and the shades of evening closed in, but Mimi did not seem to notice or to care. She sat on the floor with her arms round the body of the girl whom she loved. Darker and blacker grew the sky as the coming storm and the closing night joined forces. Still she sat on – alone – tearless – unable to think. Mimi did not know how long she sat there. Though it seemed to her that ages had passed, it could not have been more than half-an-hour. She suddenly came to herself, and was surprised to find that her grandfather had not returned. For a while she lay quiet, thinking of the immediate past. Lilla's hand was still in hers, and to her surprise it was still warm. Somehow this helped her consciousness, and without any special act of will she stood up. She lit a lamp and looked at her cousin. There was no doubt that Lilla was dead; but when the lamp-light fell on her eyes, they seemed to look at Mimi with intent – with meaning. In this state of dark isolation a new resolution came to her, and grew and grew until it became a fixed definite purpose. She would face Caswall and call him to account for his murder of Lilla – that was what she called it to herself. She would also take steps – she knew not what or how – to avenge the part taken by Lady Arabella.

In this frame of mind she lit all the lamps in the room, got water and linen from her room, and set about the decent ordering of Lilla's body. This took some time; but when it was finished, she put on her hat and cloak, put out the lights, and set out quietly for Castra Regis.

As Mimi drew near the Castle, she saw no lights except those in and around the tower room. The lights showed her that Mr. Caswall was there, so she entered by the hall door, which as usual was open, and felt her way in the darkness up the staircase to the lobby of the room. The door was ajar, and the light from within showed brilliantly through the opening. She saw Edgar Caswall walking restlessly to and fro in the room, with his hands clasped behind his back. She opened the door without knocking, and walked right into the room. As she entered, he ceased walking, and stared at her in surprise. She made no remark, no comment, but continued the fixed look which he had seen on her entrance.

For a time silence reigned, and the two stood looking fixedly at each other. Mimi was the first to speak.

"You murderer! Lilla is dead!"

"Dead! Good God! When did she die?"

"She died this afternoon, just after you left her."

"Are you sure?"

"Yes – and so are you – or you ought to be. You killed her!"

"I killed her! Be careful what you say!"

"As God sees us, it is true; and you know it. You came to Mercy Farm on purpose to break her – if you could. And the accomplice of your guilt, Lady Arabella March, came for the same purpose."

"Be careful, woman," he said hotly. "Do not use such names in that way, or you shall suffer for it."

"I am suffering for it – have suffered for it – shall suffer for it. Not for speaking the truth as I have done, but because you two, with devilish malignity, did my darling to death. It is you and your accomplice who have to dread punishment, not I."

"Take care!" he said again.

"Oh, I am not afraid of you or your accomplice," she answered spiritedly. "I am content to stand by every word I have said, every act I have done. Moreover, I believe in God's justice. I fear not the grinding of His mills; if necessary I shall set the wheels in motion myself. But you don't care for God, or believe in Him. Your god is your great kite, which cows the birds of a whole district. But be sure that His hand, when it rises, always falls at the appointed time. It may be that your name is being called even at this very moment at the Great Assize. Repent while there is still time. Happy you, if you may be allowed to enter those mighty halls in the company of the pure-souled angel whose voice has only to whisper one word of justice, and you disappear for ever into everlasting torment."

The sudden death of Lilla caused consternation among Mimi's friends and well-wishers. Such a tragedy was totally unexpected, as Adam and Sir Nathaniel had been expecting the White Worm's vengeance to fall upon themselves.

Adam, leaving his wife free to follow her own desires with regard to Lilla and her grandfather, busied himself with filling the well-hole with the fine sand prepared for the purpose, taking care to have lowered at stated intervals quantities of the store of dynamite, so as to be ready for the final explosion. He had under his immediate supervision a corps of workmen, and was assisted by Sir Nathaniel, who had come over for the purpose, and all were now staying at Lesser Hill.

Mr. Salton, too, showed much interest in the job, and was constantly coming in and out, nothing escaping his observation.

Since her marriage to Adam and their coming to stay at Doom Tower, Mimi had been fettered by fear of the horrible monster at Diana's Grove. But now she dreaded it no longer. She accepted the fact of its assuming at will the form of Lady Arabella. She had still to tax and upbraid her for her part in the unhappiness which had been wrought on Lilla, and for her share in causing her death.

One evening, when Mimi entered her own room, she went to the window and threw an eager look round the whole circle of sight. A single glance satisfied her that the White Worm in *propria persona* was not visible. So she sat down in the window-seat and enjoyed the pleasure of a full view, from which she had been so long cut off. The maid who waited on her had told her that Mr. Salton had not yet returned home, so she felt free to enjoy the luxury of peace and quiet.

As she looked out of the window, she saw something thin and white move along the avenue. She thought she recognised the figure of Lady Arabella, and instinctively drew back behind the curtain. When she had ascertained, by peeping out several times, that the lady had not seen her, she watched more carefully, all her instinctive hatred flooding back at the sight of her. Lady Arabella was moving swiftly and stealthily, looking back and around her at intervals, as if she feared to be followed. This gave Mimi an idea that she was up to no good, so she determined to seize the occasion for watching her in more detail.

Hastily putting on a dark cloak and hat, she ran downstairs and out into the avenue. Lady Arabella had moved, but the sheen of her white dress was still to be seen among the young oaks around the gateway. Keeping in shadow, Mimi followed, taking care not to come so close as to awake the other's suspicion, and watched her quarry pass along the road in the direction of Castra Regis.

She followed on steadily through the gloom of the trees, depending on the glint of the white dress to keep her right. The wood began to thicken, and presently, when the road widened and the trees grew farther back, she lost sight of any indication of her whereabouts. Under the present conditions it was impossible for her to do any more, so, after waiting for a while, still hidden in the shadow to see if she could catch another glimpse of the white frock, she determined to go on slowly towards Castra Regis, and trust to the chapter of accidents to pick up the trail again. She went on slowly, taking advantage of every obstacle and shadow to keep herself concealed.

At last she entered on the grounds of the Castle, at a spot from which the windows of the turret were dimly visible, without having seen again any sign of Lady Arabella.

Meanwhile, during most of the time that Mimi Salton had been moving warily along in the gloom, she was in reality being followed by Lady Arabella, who had caught sight of her leaving the house and had never again lost touch with her. It was a case of the hunter being hunted. For a time Mimi's many turnings, with the natural obstacles that were perpetually intervening, caused Lady Arabella some trouble; but when she was close to Castra Regis, there was no more possibility of concealment, and the strange double following went swiftly on.

When she saw Mimi close to the hall door of Castra Regis and ascending the steps, she followed. When Mimi entered the dark hall and felt her way up the staircase, still, as she believed, following Lady Arabella, the latter kept on her way. When they reached the lobby of the turret-rooms, Mimi believed that the object of her search was ahead of her.

Edgar Caswall sat in the gloom of the great room, occasionally stirred to curiosity when the drifting clouds allowed a little light to fall from the storm-swept sky. But nothing really interested him now. Since he had heard of Lilla's death, the gloom of his remorse, emphasised by Mimi's upbraiding, had made more hopeless his cruel, selfish, saturnine nature. He heard no sound, for his normal faculties seemed benumbed.

Mimi, when she came to the door, which stood ajar, gave a light tap. So light was it that it did not reach Caswall's ears. Then, taking her courage in both hands, she boldly pushed the door and entered. As she did so, her heart sank, for now she was face to face with a difficulty which had not, in her state of mental perturbation, occurred to her.

CHAPTER XXVII

ON THE TURRET ROOF

THE STORM WHICH WAS COMING was already making itself manifest, not only in the wide scope of nature, but in the hearts and natures of human beings. Electrical disturbance in the sky and the air is reproduced in animals of all kinds, and particularly in the highest type of them all – the most receptive – the most electrical. So it was with Edgar Caswall, despite his selfish nature and coldness of blood. So it was with Mimi Salton, despite her unselfish, unchanging devotion for those she loved. So it was even with Lady Arabella, who, under the instincts of a primeval serpent, carried the ever-varying wishes and customs of womanhood, which is always old – and always new.

Edgar, after he had turned his eyes on Mimi, resumed his apathetic position and sullen silence. Mimi quietly took a seat a little way apart, whence she could look on the progress of the coming storm and study its appearance throughout the whole visible circle of the neighbourhood. She was in brighter and better spirits than she had been for many days past. Lady Arabella tried to efface herself behind the now open door.

Without, the clouds grew thicker and blacker as the storm-centre came closer. As yet the forces, from whose linking the lightning springs, were held apart, and the silence of nature proclaimed the calm before the storm. Caswall felt the effect of the gathering electric force. A sort of wild exultation grew upon him, such as he had sometimes felt just before the breaking of a tropical storm. As he became conscious of this, he raised his head and caught sight of Mimi. He was in the grip of an emotion greater than himself; in the mood in which he was he felt the need upon him of doing some desperate deed. He was now absolutely reckless, and as Mimi was associated with him in the memory which drove him on, he wished that she too should be engaged in this enterprise. He had no knowledge of the proximity of Lady Arabella, and thought that he was far removed from all he knew and whose interests he shared – alone with the wild elements, which were being lashed to fury, and with the woman who had struggled with him and vanquished him, and on whom he would shower the full measure of his hate.

The fact was that Edgar Caswall was, if not mad, close to the border-line. Madness in its first stage – monomania – is a lack of proportion. So long as this is general, it is not always noticeable, for the uninspired onlooker is without the necessary means of comparison. But in monomania the errant faculty protrudes itself in a way that may not be denied. It puts aside, obscures, or takes the place of something else – just as the head of a pin placed before the centre of the iris will block out the whole scope of vision. The most usual form of monomania has commonly the same beginning as that from which Edgar Caswall suffered – an over-large idea of self-importance. Alienists, who study the matter exactly, probably know more of human vanity and its effects than do ordinary men. Caswall's mental disturbance was not hard to identify. Every asylum is full of such cases – men and women, who, naturally selfish and egotistical, so appraise to themselves their own importance that every other circumstance in life becomes subservient to it. The disease supplies in itself the material for self-magnification. When the decadence attacks a nature naturally proud and selfish and vain, and lacking both the aptitude and habit of self-restraint, the development of the disease is more swift, and ranges to farther limits. It is such persons who become inbued with the idea that they have the attributes of the Almighty – even that they themselves are the Almighty.

Mimi had a suspicion – or rather, perhaps, an intuition – of the true state of things when she heard him speak, and at the same time noticed the abnormal flush on his face, and his rolling eyes. There was a certain want of fixedness of purpose which she had certainly not noticed before – a quick, spasmodic utterance which belongs rather to the insane than to those of intellectual equilibrium. She was a little frightened, not only by his thoughts, but by his staccato way of expressing them.

Caswall moved to the door leading to the turret stair by which the roof was reached, and spoke in a peremptory way, whose tone alone made her feel defiant.

"Come! I want you."

She instinctively drew back – she was not accustomed to such words, more especially to such a tone. Her answer was indicative of a new contest.

"Why should I go? What for?"

He did not at once reply – another indication of his overwhelming egotism. She repeated her questions; habit reasserted itself, and he spoke without thinking the words which were in his heart.

"I want you, if you will be so good, to come with me to the turret roof. I am much interested in certain experiments with the kite, which would be, if not a pleasure, at least a novel experience to you. You would see something not easily seen otherwise."

"I will come," she answered simply; Edgar moved in the direction of the stair, she following close behind him.

She did not like to be left alone at such a height, in such a place, in the darkness, with a storm about to break. Of himself she had no fear; all that had been seemed to have passed away with her two victories over him in the struggle of wills. Moreover, the more recent apprehension – that of his madness – had also ceased. In the conversation of the last few minutes he seemed so rational, so clear, so unaggressive, that she no longer saw reason for doubt. So satisfied was she that even when he put out a hand to guide her to the steep, narrow stairway, she took it without thought in the most conventional way.

Lady Arabella, crouching in the lobby behind the door, heard every word that had been said, and formed her own opinion of it. It seemed evident to her that there had been some rapprochement between the two who had so lately been hostile to each other, and that made her furiously angry. Mimi was interfering with her plans! She had made certain of her capture of Edgar Caswall, and she could not tolerate even the lightest and most contemptuous fancy on his part which might divert him from the main issue. When she became aware that he wished Mimi to come with him to the roof and that she had acquiesced, her rage got beyond bounds. She became oblivious to any danger there might be in a visit to such an exposed place at such a time, and to all lesser considerations, and made up her mind to forestall them. She stealthily and noiselessly crept through the wicket, and, ascending the stair, stepped out on the roof. It was bitterly cold, for the fierce gusts of the storm which swept round the turret drove in through every unimpeded way, whistling at the sharp corners and singing round the trembling flagstaff. The kite-string and the wire which controlled the runners made a concourse of weird sounds which somehow, perhaps from the violence which surrounded them, acting on their length, resolved themselves into some kind of harmony – a fitting accompaniment to the tragedy which seemed about to begin.

Mimi's heart beat heavily. Just before leaving the turret-chamber she had a shock which she could not shake off. The lights of the room had momentarily revealed to her, as they passed out, Edgar's face, concentrated as it was whenever he intended to use his mesmeric power. Now the black eyebrows made a thick line across his face, under which his eyes shone and glittered ominously. Mimi recognised the danger, and assumed the defiant attitude that had twice already served her so well. She had a fear that the circumstances and the place were against her, and she wanted to be forearmed.

The sky was now somewhat lighter than it had been. Either there was lightning afar off, whose reflections were carried by the rolling clouds, or else the gathered force, though not yet breaking into lightning, had an incipient power of light. It seemed to affect both the man and the woman. Edgar seemed altogether under its influence. His spirits were boisterous, his mind exalted. He was now at his worst; madder than he had been earlier in the night.

Mimi, trying to keep as far from him as possible, moved across the stone floor of the turret roof, and found a niche which concealed her. It was not far from Lady Arabella's place of hiding.

Edgar, left thus alone on the centre of the turret roof, found himself altogether his own master in a way which tended to increase his madness. He knew that Mimi was close at hand, though he had lost sight of her. He spoke loudly, and the sound of his own voice, though it was carried from him on the sweeping wind as fast as the words were spoken, seemed to exalt him still more. Even the raging of the elements round him appeared to add to his exaltation. To him it seemed that these manifestations were obedient to his own will. He had reached the sublime of his madness; he was now in his own mind actually the Almighty, and whatever might happen would be the direct carrying out of his own commands. As he could not see Mimi, nor fix whereabout she was, he shouted loudly:

"Come to me! You shall see now what you are despising, what you are warring against. All that you see is mine – the darkness as well as the light. I tell you that I am greater than any other who is, or was, or shall be. When the Master of Evil took Christ up on a high place and showed Him all the kingdoms of the earth, he was doing what he thought no other could do. He was wrong – he forgot *me*. I shall send you light, up to the very ramparts of heaven. A light so great that it shall dissipate those black clouds that are rushing up and piling around us. Look! Look! At the very touch of my hand that light springs into being and mounts up – and up – and up!"

He made his way whilst he was speaking to the corner of the turret whence flew the giant kite, and from which the runners ascended. Mimi looked on, appalled and afraid to speak lest she should precipitate some calamity. Within the niche Lady Arabella cowered in a paroxysm of fear.

Edgar took up a small wooden box, through a hole in which the wire of the runner ran. This evidently set some machinery in motion, for a sound as of whirring came. From one side of the box floated what looked like a piece of stiff ribbon, which snapped and crackled as the wind took it. For a few seconds Mimi saw it as it rushed along the sagging line to the kite. When close to it, there was a loud crack, and a sudden light appeared to issue from every chink in the box. Then a quick flame flashed along the snapping ribbon, which glowed with an intense light – a light so great that the whole of the countryside around stood out against the background of black driving clouds. For a few seconds the light remained, then suddenly disappeared in the blackness around. It was simply a magnesium light, which had been fired by the mechanism within the box and carried up to the kite. Edgar was in a state of tumultuous excitement, shouting and yelling at the top of his voice and dancing about like a lunatic.

This was more than Lady Arabella's curious dual nature could stand – the ghoulish element in her rose triumphant, and she abandoned all idea of marriage with Edgar Caswall, gloating fiendishly over the thought of revenge.

She must lure him to the White Worm's hole – but how? She glanced around and quickly made up her mind. The man's whole thoughts were absorbed by his wonderful kite, which he was showing off, in order to fascinate her imaginary rival, Mimi.

On the instant she glided through the darkness to the wheel whereon the string of the kite was wound. With deft fingers she unshipped this, took it with her, reeling out the wire as she went, thus keeping, in a way, in touch with the kite. Then she glided swiftly to the wicket, through which she passed, locking the gate behind her as she went.

Down the turret stair she ran quickly, letting the wire run from the wheel which she carried carefully, and, passing out of the hall door, hurried down the avenue with all her speed. She soon reached her own gate, ran down the avenue, and with her key opened the iron door leading to the well-hole.

She felt well satisfied with herself. All her plans were maturing, or had already matured. The Master of Castra Regis was within her grasp. The woman whose interference she had feared, Lilla Watford, was dead. Truly, all was well, and she felt that she might pause a while and rest. She tore off her clothes, with feverish fingers, and in full enjoyment of her natural freedom, stretched her slim figure in animal delight. Then she lay down on the sofa – to await her victim! Edgar Caswall's life blood would more than satisfy her for some time to come.

CHAPTER XXVIII

THE BREAKING OF THE STORM

WHEN LADY ARABELLA HAD crept away in her usual noiseless fashion, the two others remained for a while in their places on the turret roof: Caswall because he had nothing to say, Mimi because she had much to say and wished to put her thoughts in order. For quite a while – which seemed interminable – silence reigned between them. At last Mimi made a beginning – she had made up her mind how to act.

"Mr. Caswall," she said loudly, so as to make sure of being heard through the blustering of the wind and the perpetual cracking of the electricity.

Caswall said something in reply, but his words were carried away on the storm. However, one of her objects was effected: she knew now exactly whereabout on the roof he was. So she moved close to the spot before she spoke again, raising her voice almost to a shout.

"The wicket is shut. Please to open it. I can't get out."

As she spoke, she was quietly fingering a revolver which Adam had given to her in case of emergency and which now lay in her breast. She felt that she was caged like a rat in a trap, but did not mean to be taken at a disadvantage, whatever happened. Caswall also felt trapped, and all the brute in him rose to the emergency. In a voice which was raucous and brutal – much like that which is heard when a wife is being beaten by her husband in a slum – he hissed out, his syllables cutting through the roaring of the storm:

"You came of your own accord – without permission, or even asking it. Now you can stay or go as you choose. But you must manage it for yourself; I'll have nothing to do with it."

Her answer was spoken with dangerous suavity

"I am going. Blame yourself if you do not like the time and manner of it. I daresay Adam – my husband – will have a word to say to you about it!"

"Let him say, and be damned to him, and to you too! I'll show you a light. You shan't be able to say that you could not see what you were doing."

As he spoke, he was lighting another piece of the magnesium ribbon, which made a blinding glare in which everything was plainly discernible, down to the smallest detail. This exactly suited Mimi. She took accurate note of the wicket and its fastening before the glare had died away. She took her revolver out and fired into the lock, which was shivered on the instant, the pieces flying round in all directions, but happily without causing hurt to anyone. Then she pushed the wicket open and ran down the narrow stair, and so to the hall door. Opening this also, she ran down the avenue, never lessening her speed till she stood outside the door of Lesser Hill. The door was opened at once on her ringing.

"Is Mr. Adam Salton in?" she asked.

"He has just come in, a few minutes ago. He has gone up to the study," replied a servant.

She ran upstairs at once and joined him. He seemed relieved when he saw her, but scrutinised her face keenly. He saw that she had been in some concern, so led her over to the sofa in the window and sat down beside her.

"Now, dear, tell me all about it!" he said.

She rushed breathlessly through all the details of her adventure on the turret roof. Adam listened attentively, helping her all he could, and not embarrassing her by any questioning. His thoughtful silence was a great help to her, for it allowed her to collect and organise her thoughts.

"I must go and see Caswall to-morrow, to hear what he has to say on the subject."

"But, dear, for my sake, don't have any quarrel with Mr. Caswall. I have had too much trial and pain lately to wish it increased by any anxiety regarding you."

"You shall not, dear – if I can help it – please God," he said solemnly, and he kissed her.

Then, in order to keep her interested so that she might forget the fears and anxieties that had disturbed her, he began to talk over the details of her adventure, making shrewd comments which attracted and held her attention. Presently, *inter alia*, he said:

"That's a dangerous game Caswall is up to. It seems to me that that young man – though he doesn't appear to know it – is riding for a fall!"

"How, dear? I don't understand."

"Kite flying on a night like this from a place like the tower of Castra Regis is, to say the least of it, dangerous. It is not merely courting death or other accident from lightning, but it is bringing the lightning into where he lives. Every cloud that is blowing up here – and they all make for the highest point – is bound to develop into a flash of lightning. That kite is up in the air and is bound to attract the lightning. Its cord makes a road for it on which to travel to earth. When it does come, it will strike the top of the tower with a weight a hundred times greater than a whole park of artillery, and will knock Castra Regis into pieces. Where it will go after that, no one can tell. If there should be any metal by which it can travel, such will not only point the road, but be the road itself."

"Would it be dangerous to be out in the open air when such a thing is taking place?" she asked.

"No, little woman. It would be the safest possible place – so long as one was not in the line of the electric current."

"Then, do let us go outside. I don't want to run into any foolish danger – or, far more, to ask you to do so. But surely if the open is safest, that is the place for us."

Without another word, she put on again the cloak she had thrown off, and a small, tight-fitting cap. Adam too put on his cap, and, after seeing that his revolver was all right, gave her his hand, and they left the house together.

"I think the best thing we can do will be to go round all the places which are mixed up in this affair."

"All right, dear, I am ready. But, if you don't mind, we might go first to Mercy. I am anxious about grandfather, and we might see that – as yet, at all events – nothing has happened there."

So they went on the high-hung road along the top of the Brow.

The wind here was of great force, and made a strange booming noise as it swept high overhead; though not the sound of cracking and tearing as it passed through the woods of high slender trees which grew on either side of the road. Mimi could hardly keep her feet. She was not afraid; but the force to which she was opposed gave her a good excuse to hold on to her husband extra tight.

At Mercy there was no one up – at least, all the lights were out. But to Mimi, accustomed to the nightly routine of the house, there were manifest signs that all was well, except in the little room on the first floor, where the blinds were down. Mimi could not bear to look at that, to think of it. Adam understood her pain, for he had been keenly interested in poor Lilla. He bent over and kissed her, and then took her hand and held it hard. Thus they passed on together, returning to the high road towards Castra Regis.

At the gate of Castra Regis they were extra careful. When drawing near, Adam stumbled upon the wire that Lady Arabella had left trailing on the ground.

Adam drew his breath at this, and spoke in a low, earnest whisper:

"I don't want to frighten you, Mimi dear, but wherever that wire is there is danger."

"Danger! How?"

"That is the track where the lightning will go; at any moment, even now whilst we are speaking and searching, a fearful force may be loosed upon us. Run on, dear; you know the way to where the avenue joins the highroad. If you see any sign of the wire, keep away from it, for God's sake. I shall join you at the gateway."

"Are you going to follow that wire alone?"

"Yes, dear. One is sufficient for that work. I shall not lose a moment till I am with you."

"Adam, when I came with you into the open, my main wish was that we should be together if anything serious happened. You wouldn't deny me that right, would you, dear?"

"No, dear, not that or any right. Thank God that my wife has such a wish. Come; we will go together. We are in the hands of God. If He wishes, we shall be together at the end, whenever or wherever that may be."

They picked up the trail of the wire on the steps and followed it down the avenue, taking care not to touch it with their feet. It was easy enough to follow, for the wire, if not bright, was self-coloured, and showed clearly. They followed it out of the gateway and into the avenue of Diana's Grove.

Here a new gravity clouded Adam's face, though Mimi saw no cause for fresh concern. This was easily enough explained. Adam knew of the explosive works in progress regarding the well-hole, but the matter had been kept from his wife. As they stood near the house, Adam asked Mimi to return to the road, ostensibly to watch the course of the wire, telling her that there might be a branch wire leading somewhere else. She was to search the undergrowth, and if she found it, was to warn him by the Australian native "Coo-ee!"

Whilst they were standing together, there came a blinding flash of lightning, which lit up for several seconds the whole area of earth and sky. It was only the first note of the celestial prelude, for it was followed in quick succession by numerous flashes, whilst the crash and roll of thunder seemed continuous.

Adam, appalled, drew his wife to him and held her close. As far as he could estimate by the interval between lightning and thunder-clap, the heart of the storm was still some distance off, so he felt no present concern for their safety. Still, it was apparent that the course of the storm was moving swiftly in their direction. The lightning flashes came faster and faster and closer together; the thunder-roll was almost continuous, not stopping for a moment — a new crash beginning before the old one had ceased. Adam kept looking up in the direction where the kite strained and struggled at its detaining cord, but, of course, the dull evening light prevented any distinct scrutiny.

At length there came a flash so appallingly bright that in its glare Nature seemed to be standing still. So long did it last, that there was time to distinguish its configuration. It seemed like a mighty tree inverted, pendent from the sky. The whole country around within the angle of vision was lit up till it seemed to glow. Then a broad ribbon of fire seemed to drop on to the tower of Castra Regis just as the thunder crashed. By the glare, Adam could see the tower shake and tremble, and finally fall to pieces like a house of cards. The passing of the lightning left the sky again dark, but a blue flame fell downward from the tower, and, with inconceivable rapidity, running along the ground in the direction of Diana's Grove, reached the dark silent house, which in the instant burst into flame at a hundred different points.

At the same moment there rose from the house a rending, crashing sound of woodwork, broken or thrown about, mixed with a quick scream so appalling that Adam, stout of heart as he undoubtedly was, felt his blood turn into ice. Instinctively, despite the danger and their consciousness of it, husband and wife took hands and listened, trembling. Something was going on close to them, mysterious, terrible, deadly! The shrieks continued, though less sharp in sound, as though muffled. In the midst of them was a terrific explosion, seemingly from deep in the earth.

The flames from Castra Regis and from Diana's Grove made all around almost as light as day, and now that the lightning had ceased to flash, their eyes, unblinded, were able to judge both perspective and detail. The heat of the burning house caused the iron doors to warp and collapse. Seemingly of their own accord, they fell open, and exposed the interior. The Saltons could now look through to the room beyond, where the well-hole yawned, a deep narrow circular chasm. From this the agonised shrieks were rising, growing ever more terrible with each second that passed.

But it was not only the heart-rending sound that almost paralysed poor Mimi with terror. What she saw was sufficient to fill her with evil dreams for the remainder of her life. The whole place looked as if a sea of blood had been beating against it. Each of the explosions from below had thrown out from the well-hole, as if it had been the mouth of a cannon, a mass of fine sand mixed with blood, and a horrible repulsive slime in which were great red masses of rent and torn flesh and fat. As the explosions kept on, more and more of this repulsive mass was shot up, the great bulk of it falling back again. Many of the awful fragments were of something which had lately been alive. They quivered and trembled and writhed as though they were still in torment, a supposition to which the unending scream gave a horrible credence. At moments some mountainous mass of flesh surged up through the narrow orifice, as though forced by a measureless power through an opening infinitely smaller than itself. Some of these fragments were partially covered with white skin as of a human being, and others – the largest and most numerous – with scaled skin as of a gigantic lizard or serpent. Once, in a sort of lull or pause, the seething contents of the hole rose, after the manner of a bubbling spring, and Adam saw part of the thin form of Lady Arabella, forced up to the top amid a mass of blood and slime, and what looked as if it had been the entrails of a monster torn into shreds. Several times some masses of enormous bulk were forced up through the well-hole with inconceivable violence, and, suddenly expanding as they came into larger space, disclosed sections of the White Worm which Adam and Sir Nathaniel had seen looking over the trees with its enormous eyes of emerald-green flickering like great lamps in a gale.

At last the explosive power, which was not yet exhausted, evidently reached the main store of dynamite which had been lowered into the worm hole. The result was appalling. The ground for far around quivered and opened in long deep chasms, whose edges shook and fell in, throwing up clouds of sand which fell back and hissed amongst the rising water. The heavily built house shook to its foundations. Great stones were thrown up as from a volcano, some of them, great masses of hard stone, squared and grooved with implements wrought by human hands, breaking up and splitting in mid air as though riven by some infernal power. Trees near the house – and therefore presumably in some way above the hole, which sent up clouds of dust and steam and fine sand mingled, and which carried an appalling stench which sickened the spectators – were torn up by the roots and hurled into the air. By now, flames were bursting violently from all over the ruins, so dangerously that Adam caught up his wife in his arms, and ran with her from the proximity of the flames.

Then almost as quickly as it had begun, the whole cataclysm ceased, though a deep-down rumbling continued intermittently for some time. Then silence brooded over all – silence so complete that it seemed in itself a sentient thing – silence which seemed like incarnate darkness, and conveyed the same idea to all who came within its radius. To the young people who had suffered the long horror of that awful night, it brought relief – relief from the presence or the fear of all that was horrible – relief which seemed perfected when the red rays of sunrise shot up over the far eastern sea, bringing a promise of a new order of things with the coming day.

His bed saw little of Adam Salton for the remainder of that night. He and Mimi walked hand in hand in the brightening dawn round by the Brow to Castra Regis and on to Lesser Hill. They did so deliberately, in an attempt to think as little as possible of the terrible experiences of the night. The morning was bright and cheerful, as a morning sometimes is after a devastating storm. The clouds, of which there were plenty in evidence, brought no lingering idea of gloom. All nature was bright and joyous, being in striking contrast to the scenes of wreck and devastation, the effects of obliterating fire and lasting ruin.

The only evidence of the once stately pile of Castra Regis and its inhabitants was a shapeless huddle of shattered architecture, dimly seen as the keen breeze swept aside the cloud of acrid smoke which marked the site of the once lordly castle. As for Diana's Grove, they looked in vain for a sign which had a suggestion of permanence. The oak trees of the Grove were still to be seen – some of them – emerging from a haze of smoke, the great trunks solid and erect as ever, but the larger branches broken and twisted and rent, with bark stripped and chipped, and the smaller branches broken and dishevelled looking from the constant stress and threshing of the storm.

Of the house as such, there was, even at the short distance from which they looked, no trace. Adam resolutely turned his back on the devastation and hurried on. Mimi was not only upset and shocked in many ways, but she was physically "dog tired," and falling asleep on her feet. Adam took her to her room and made her undress and get into bed, taking care that the room was well lighted both by sunshine and lamps. The only obstruction was from a silk curtain, drawn across the window to keep out the glare. He sat beside her, holding her hand, well knowing that the comfort of his presence was the best restorative for her. He stayed with her till sleep had overmastered her wearied body. Then he went softly away. He found his uncle and Sir Nathaniel in the study, having an early cup of tea, amplified to the dimensions of a possible breakfast. Adam explained that he had not told his wife that he was going over the horrible places again, lest it should frighten her, for the rest and sleep in ignorance would help her and make a gap of peacefulness between the horrors.

Sir Nathaniel agreed.

"We know, my boy," he said, "that the unfortunate Lady Arabella is dead, and that the foul carcase of the Worm has been torn to pieces – pray God that its evil soul will never more escape from the nethermost hell."

They visited Diana's Grove first, not only because it was nearer, but also because it was the place where most description was required, and Adam felt that he could tell his story best on the spot. The absolute destruction of the place and everything in it seen in the broad daylight was almost inconceivable. To Sir Nathaniel, it was as a story of horror full and complete. But to Adam it was, as it were, only on the fringes. He knew what was still to be seen when his friends had got over the knowledge of externals. As yet, they had only seen the outside of the house – or rather, where the outside of the house once had been. The great horror lay within. However, age – and the experience of age – counts.

A strange, almost elemental, change in the aspect had taken place in the time which had elapsed since the dawn. It would almost seem as if Nature herself had tried to obliterate the evil signs of what had occurred. True, the utter ruin of the house was made even more manifest in the searching daylight; but the more appalling destruction which lay beneath was not visible. The rent, torn, and dislocated stonework looked worse than before; the upheaved foundations, the piled-up fragments of masonry, the fissures in the torn earth – all were at the worst. The Worm's hole was still evident, a round fissure seemingly leading down into the very bowels of the earth. But all the horrid mass of blood and slime, of torn, evil-smelling flesh and the sickening remnants of violent death, were gone. Either some of the later explosions had thrown up from the deep quantities of water which, though foul and corrupt itself, had still some cleansing power left, or else the writhing mass which stirred from far below had helped to drag down and obliterate the items of horror. A grey dust, partly of fine sand, partly of the waste of the falling ruin, covered everything, and, though ghastly itself, helped to mask something still worse.

After a few minutes of watching, it became apparent to the three men that the turmoil far below had not yet ceased. At short irregular intervals the hell-broth in the hole seemed as if boiling up. It rose and fell again and turned over, showing in fresh form much of the nauseous detail which had been visible earlier. The worst parts were the great masses of the flesh of the monstrous Worm, in all its red and sickening aspect. Such fragments had been bad enough before, but now they were infinitely worse. Corruption comes with startling rapidity to beings whose destruction has been due wholly or in part to lightning – the whole mass seemed to have become all at once corrupt! The whole surface of the fragments, once alive, was covered with insects, worms, and vermin of all kinds. The sight was horrible enough, but, with the awful smell added, was simply unbearable. The Worm's hole appeared to breathe forth death in its most repulsive forms. The friends, with one impulse, moved to the top of the Brow, where a fresh breeze from the sea was blowing up.

At the top of the Brow, beneath them as they looked down, they saw a shining mass of white, which looked strangely out of place amongst such wreckage as they had been viewing. It appeared so strange that Adam suggested trying to find a way down, so that they might see it more closely.

"We need not go down; I know what it is," Sir Nathaniel said. "The explosions of last night have blown off the outside of the cliffs – that which we see is the vast bed of china clay through which the Worm originally found its way down to its lair. I can catch the glint of the water of the deep quags far down below. Well, her ladyship didn't deserve such a funeral – or such a monument."

The horrors of the last few hours had played such havoc with Mimi's nerves, that a change of scene was imperative – if a permanent breakdown was to be avoided.

"I think," said old Mr. Salton, "it is quite time you young people departed for that honeymoon of yours!" There was a twinkle in his eye as he spoke.

Mimi's soft shy glance at her stalwart husband, was sufficient answer.

Publisher's Note

Bram Stoker was a man of his time, a fact often betrayed in the language he used in writing Lair of the White Worm. This was a world with strong racist underpinnings and an unshakeable belief, at least by Europeans and their descendants, in their superiority over the other peoples of the Earth. It seems to have been widely unquestioned that there were absolute differences in the capabilities and value of human beings dependent entirely upon their ethnicity or, as Stoker and other writers of his time would have put it, 'race'. This world view has long since become obsolete and is indeed shocking to contemporary tastes. It seems incredible now that any writer could seriously have chosen to have his heroes and heroines refer to another, admittedly wicked, character as a 'nigger' without a trace of irony. Because the world has changed since Stoker wrote this book, the liberal sprinklings of this nowadays racist and ugly word have largely been removed from this edition and replaced with terms which attempt to remain in harmony with this period piece without unnecessarily inflaming the modern reader's outrage. It is hoped that readers will agree that this does no serious injury to the book. It is certainly the editor's opinion that Stoker would not have deliberately attempted to put his readers offside of his most sympathetic characters by making them appear as racist buffoons. However, this is not an editorial consideration that was extended to the villains! For those readers that are interested in such details or who prefer their fiction in its undiluted and original form, the words that have been altered are each marked with a superscript asterisk (*).

Search Amazon.com or Barnes and Noble for other Fantasy and
Science Fiction books available from Deodand Books by ISBN:

A PRINCESS OF MARS
EDGAR RICE BURROUGHS
ISBN: 0957886853

WHEN ALL MOONS RISE
ANDREW CHAPMAN
ISBN: 0957886829

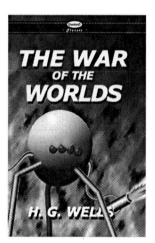

THE WAR OF THE WORLDS
H.G. WELLS
ISBN: 0957886861

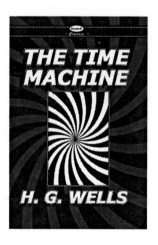

THE TIME MACHINE

Printed in the United Kingdom
by Lightning Source UK Ltd.
132701UK00001B/36/A